Scarce Resources

18 Weird Stories
by Brendan Detzner

"Quiet" originally appeared in Ruthless Peoples
"Ducks" originally appeared in Edge of Propinquity
"Dinosaurs" originally appeared in Chizine
"Veronica" originally appeared in Untied Shoelaces of the Mind
"Iowa Highway" originally appeared in Pseudopod
"Rolling Bones" originally appeared in Gothic.net

Table of Contents

The Black Plague

1

I go straight to the theater from the shed, still smelling like grass clippings. I think about driving home to take a shower and coming straight back, but I don't want to wait. She says she likes the way I smell. I believe everything that she tells me, every word that comes out of her mouth. All day I've been walking behind the lawnmower, thinking about when I'll have everything done and I'll be able to see her again. I trust her so completely that I stand at a distance from myself like a ghost and wonder how this is happening.

I walk around the far end of the building, the side opposite the main entrance where the patrons aren't allowed to go. There's a bank of windows on the wall facing the sidewalk that leads to the maintenance entrance. I can see the costume shop, a half a dozen thick wooden tables with white sewing machines attached to them and giant rolls of fabric mounted on the walls. The light from the hallway lamps makes everything look yellow. Only Karen and Liz are in the shop. I am amazed that I remember their names. They are working on opposite sides of the same dress, leaning in close and whispering to each other. They glance at me and giggle; Karen waves at me as I unlock the door and come inside. Liz laughs and covers her eyes.

There I am again, standing outside of myself. I can still hear them laughing as I walk down the hall.

Harriet works in the costuming department, but she has a special job, her own room to work in. I open the door with her name on it and step inside. I am surrounded by eyes and mouths, open in surprise or twisted into a grimace. I close the door behind me. I don't see her. There is a lamp sitting on the floor, a bare light bulb.

"Come here."

I do, and there she is. She's perched on top of a long narrow worktable, wearing a cat mask decorated with blue feathers, and her own skin. Her long hair has vanished, tucked away somewhere. I see her neck, her shoulders.

I get closer. I touch the side of her body with my hand, trace her rib with my thumb and dig into her back with my fingers.

We make love. She smells really nice. She tells me what it is later, it's not perfume, it's some herbal thing. My attention wanders while she's explaining the details. She pinches me; I pinch her back. There's not enough room to wrestle, there's not even room for both of us, she's lying on top of me. We kind of squirm.

She hops down from the bench and puts her clothes on, takes off the mask and shakes her hair out. I watch her and it hurts.

She talks about what she's been working on, her latest project. There's a whole row devoted to it. They all have long pointed noses; I make a dirty joke but the time has passed and she doesn't laugh. I say something about Mardi Gras and that's better, she tells me I've got it right. These didn't used to be part of a costume. People wore them in the Middle Ages when people first started getting sick. The idea was that it would keep the bad air out. That's why they thought everybody was dying, bad air. All the faeries are going to wear them, it's supposed to represent something. The director talked to everybody about it before rehearsals started. I wasn't there for that. I just cut the grass.

The sun shines through the window. I have to go, I'm not even supposed to be here now, it's Saturday. I have weekends off, but opening night is coming soon and the crew isn't leaving the building until everything's ready for dress rehearsal. I kiss her goodbye and I head out.

2

I told myself when I got the job that it'd be a good way to clear my head for the summer and read a lot of books, but the stack next to my mattress in the room I rented has hardly been touched. I pass out without closing the shades and wake up in my clothes a few hours later with the sun shining in my face. I take a shower and go for a walk along the lake. It's a clear day, all the boats are out on the water. An elderly woman in a pink windbreaker stops me as I walk past the dock and asks for my help getting her sails tied down. I tell her that I don't know anything about boats but she doesn't believe me; I have to brush past her with my shoulders.

I buy a sandwich and devour it. I see a Midsummer flier on the bulletin board next to the door as I walk out. It's a big event; this is a family town in the summer. They do screenings of old movies in the park, concerts and picnics around the bandstand.

My phone buzzes. It's her. I sit on a rock and say that I was just thinking about her, I'm hoping that she'll like that but it doesn't even make a dent; she's really upset and won't tell me why, she says she just wants to hear my voice. I tell her I'm going to go see her. She tells me I can't. I hang up on her and jog back the same way I just walked.

The theater building used to be the main house of a very rich man's estate. The paths leading to it weave back and forth through flower gardens and sculptures. I can hear the director yelling; he stops and everything is quiet. The speakers hanging above the stage kick my ears as they're turned on. I hear amplified voices, calm and in character in spite of whatever it was that just happened.

I hesitate before I turn the corner. I'm not supposed to be here. The rehearsals have been closed since they began and the director is an asshole.

I turn away and walk back towards the building. A door is propped open and I go through it. When I come back out I'm wearing a black robe and a mask with a long nose. I approach the stage again, turning the corner. There are people wandering around quietly, waiting for their turn

3

to come up, some of them entirely in costume and others only partially. Harriet is set up next to an oak tree to the right of the stage. She's spinning around like she's broken; for every mask she hands out, she picks up two and has to remember where they came from.

I wait until they leave, then I come up behind her and put my hand on her shoulder. She turns around like she's going to hit me; I whisper her name and she almost collapses onto the grass.

She pulls me towards a clearing where nobody can see us. I take my mask off and kiss her on the cheek. She tells me she's glad I'm here and starts crying.

It wasn't anything all that bad, the director yelled at some guy and he yelled at Harriet and said the mistake was her fault somehow. Stuff like that gets to her really easily. It's kind of a big deal for her to be living out here by herself, even just for a couple of months. It's a big deal for her to be with me, too, and for me to be with her. Girls don't like me, usually.

She feels better now. I tell her that I'm going to try and be around as often as I can. She goes back to work. I put my mask back on and stand under her tree for the rest of the afternoon.

3

For the next few days I try to be there as much as I can. Nobody ever asks what I'm doing, I keep my face hidden and they all have other things to worry about.

Opening night comes quickly. Harriet's job is simple, she just has to keep all the costumes straight, but she's nervous. She wants me to be there. I keep the mask and the robe with me when I leave the night before, and come back early in the morning, before any of the crew have arrived. I wait in the clearing for night to come, and finally approach the stage when I hear crowd noise. Everybody else is in full costume, nobody notices me except Harriet. She squeezes my hand and smiles.

The play begins. The field in front of the stage has been filled with folding chairs and lined with white Christmas lights. Harriet doesn't make any mistakes. I watch the show. The rude mechanicals take the stage.

"Have you sent to Bottom's house? Is he come home yet?"

"He cannot be heard of. Out of doubt he is transported."

"If he come not, then the play…"

Flute starts coughing, followed very shortly by almost every one else in the garden. He collapses. A few rows of folding chairs tip over like dominos and soon the audience is all dead.

4

The first time Harriet coughs, I don't think it's a big deal. The second time, it sounds ugly, like something inside of her is getting torn up. She turns around and looks up at me, and without really thinking about what I'm doing I pick up a mask with a long nose and press it against her face. She breathes deeply and coughs again, but it's not as bad.

The only people left standing are all wearing plague masks. One of them walks out in front of the stage. She takes her mask off and I can see that she's crying. She coughs once, coughs again, falls over, coughs a few more times and stops moving. The spotlights are all pointing in different directions.

We file silently into the main building. Harriet is too weak to walk, so I carry her. People start yelling at each other as soon as the doors close. I'm mostly worried about Harriet and don't say too much, but I mention that it might be a good idea to head into the basement and close all the doors. Somebody else says the same thing, only louder. Soon we're all heading down the stairs.

We cram ourselves into the boiler room and wait silently. Somebody finally takes their mask off. They're fine. Everybody else does the same thing and we all start arguing again. The same guy from before gets control of the room somehow, he's yelling at first but brings it down once people start paying attention. He says that we've got to get organized, that we need to see what's going on outside. Somehow it becomes my job to go downtown. They tell me that Harriet will be fine, that they'll take care of her.

I put my mask back on, stop by the shed to pick up a flashlight, and walk towards the lake. The streets are empty. Boats bob up and down in the water like corks. Some of the stores have bodies slumped behind the cash register or lying on the floor. I yell a few times but nobody answers me.

The electricity still works. I see a television set playing through the window of a bar. I stop by the shed again before I go back inside and turn on the radio. There's music or commercials playing on all the FM stations, but when I turn to the talk shows I get nothing but silence.

I go back inside. Harriet's asleep, so are a few other people. No one who went out comes back with any news of human life outside of this room, but people are sure that help is coming. Not just other people, I feel that way too. There has to be somebody out there. Any minute, we expect the helicopters to land and guys in gas masks to start pouring out.

For two days, nothing like that happens. We head into town in shifts and bring back shopping carts full of canned food and camping supplies. Everyone works together, nobody argues. Nobody wants to be left without something to keep their hands busy.

Halfway through the first day, the electricity dies. People worry about the air conditioning, but it doesn't seem to make any difference when it stops working. Some of us think the reason we're still alive is because the basement is underground, that maybe whatever it is in the air rises up. Nobody knows for sure. We try not to open and close the door to the basement any more then we have to.

Harriet isn't able to do a whole lot. She's really sick, just standing up makes her dizzy. I spend as much time with her as I can, and we go to sleep every night huddled together like animals. The others avoid her.

It's strange. Nobody wants to admit how scared they are. Nobody talks about their families. The world might have ended and there are people actually smiling. Trying to cheer each other up.

And I'm doing it too, that's the fucked up thing. I'm part of the team.

5

The days go by. If nobody comes by the end of the month we've all decided to head for Milwaukee and see how things look.

One day, when I get back from town, I go down into the basement and Harriet isn't there. I ask everybody where she is. The guy who said we needed to get organized says he's got something he needs to show me. We put our masks on and go upstairs.

She's in her workshop. They've given her a mattress, a blanket, and some food. I see her through the window, sleeping in the fetal position with her mask on. The leader puts his hand on my shoulder and tells me that he understands this can't be easy for me. He doesn't say what he's worried about, not specifically. Just that she's sick and we're not.

The world flips right side up again. I try not to let it show on my face. He asks me if I understand, if I'm okay with this. I tell him that I understand. He goes back downstairs. I go outside and get a burlap sack from the shed. I fold it up and shove it into my back pocket.

They've taken one of the racks from Harriet's studio and moved it to the basement. Everybody hangs their masks there. I wait until everybody is asleep and put the masks into the sack, quietly, one at a time.

I leave the basement again, and throw the bag into a flower garden on my way to the shed. I come back with a gas can and empty it into the garden.

I light a match.

I go to Harriet's room and wake her up. She's happy to see me. I tell her we're leaving and help her to her feet. She sees the fire as we step through the doorway and looks up at me, concerned. Afraid that something's gone wrong.

Music for Scalpel and Prepared Piano

In the process of removing Susanna's eyes and tongue, he'd punctured one of her eyeballs and ripped her tongue in half. He could go without the tongue, but not the eye. He hadn't wanted to hurt Brian. Brian was his best student. But he had no choice. If he took the time to find somebody else, he might get caught before he was finished.

He'd meant to leave him alive, but he was a composer, not a surgeon.

The House Rock and Roll Built

I've tried to bullshit my way around it, but the reason I'm writing this is because I feel guilty. Probably not as much as I should be, but a little bit. Maybe if people know what happened I'll feel better. The consequences don't worry me because I don't think there'll be any, Courtney's got a good thing going in Vegas I doubt she'd want to fuck up and nobody cares about the others. They're footnotes of history, chased off the radio by shitty German keyboard music a long time ago. It took seventy or so years to kill the dragon but it's finally happened. There will be no more skinny white guys getting famous by playing guitar and screaming. It will never, ever, ever, ever happen again and I'm glad.

I've decided to come clean because I'm going to die. I was a little hazy on that when I was younger; over the course of the last few years I was coming to accept it, but all the new shit they've been talking about on television put a wrench in the works. No more dying, no more falling apart, just a shot of nanites every three weeks and a little jolt of electricity every morning to keep your brain happy. I've got a little thing that looks like a nightlight with a red bulb in my medicine cabinet. Every morning I turn it on and let my skin soak up the light, and I don't get wrinkles. Thirty years ago I'd have killed somebody in front of their mother for this thing, now I can buy it at a drugstore. So when the cover of Newsweek tells me that maybe things have changed, that maybe we're the "Generation Without Death" in big white letters, maybe I believe it.

So I go to see the doctor. I get checked over by a nurse, answer a lot of embarrassing questions about all the substances that have found their way into my body over the years, leave and come back a week later. The doctor sees me personally. He has his bad news face on. I missed the boat. If I was a little younger, if I was a little healthier, if the technology was just a little further along…

I didn't kill Kurt Cobain. But I had something to do with it.

I'd heard about the guy from maybe six different people before I ever met him. It's even possible that I'd heard his voice on the radio, that would've been right when things were getting going. I wasn't at the club to see him, I was just at the club, it was an industry thing. I wasn't really in the industry at that point, but I'd come to the west coast to work on that and I'd made enough friends to get in the door. I was backstage when I first heard his voice, laughing along with the rest of the band as a fruit basket went flying out of their dressing room. It hit the wall on the other side of the hall and landed upside down on the tile floor, sending grapes rolling all over the place.

The bald guy was at the other end of the hall. He watched the basket fly with the wide-eyed look of a puppy that's been kicked in the head by someone it loved. I'm not going to tell you the bald guy's name, there's no reason to drag him into it. He was old by the standards of the music industry. This does not mean that he was old by anybody else's standards - he wasn't really bald either, his hairline was just receding a little bit. But as far as the people he spent most of his time with were concerned, he was old and he was bald, and when he lost the job he had he wasn't likely to get another one.

He just stood there and stared at the fruit basket.

"My wife made that fruit basket," he said.

He came by and sat next to me at the bar a little later that night. We'd always gotten along, he'd always said if he had a little more pull he could get me a spot working for him. I said something that made him feel better; we shook hands before he went home. I didn't stay much longer then he did. At some point they played, but I wasn't really paying attention. They were just another band. Depending on exactly when they came on they had somewhere in between ten and twenty minutes to get my attention, and they didn't pull it off.

I heard them once more before I really knew who they were, on the radio, on a Sunday morning. That was when it soaked through a little bit, when it got me. I was driving, and the song came on, and I forgot where I was and what I was doing. Drums crashed, guitars roared, all that. Three and a half minutes seemed to take an hour to go by.

It didn't change my life, but it made things happen for me, at least for a little bit. That's not a small thing. You've got to understand, I could've done anything, it didn't have to be the music business. I make friends everywhere I go without trying, people want me to come to their parties, people want me to like them and say nice things about them. All kinds of people. I can go anywhere. I could have been polishing off my second million at that point if I'd gone into an industry that made any sense, but I like music. I like that feeling. Maybe I liked all the bullshit surrounding it too, sex and drugs and rock and roll, but that was never the whole thing.

So when I heard that song on the radio, my first reflex was to forgive him. So he threw a fruit basket. Maybe he was having a bad day, whatever. He was probably a decent guy.

Then I met him. It was three years later. Things weren't going as well for me as I'd hoped and I'd had to find ways to pay the rent that I wasn't proud of. One Sunday I got a phone call from the bald guy. I hadn't heard from him in a while.

"Look, Kurt's in L.A. and he's coming over to your place."

I thought he was bullshitting me. "Good morning."

"I don't have any time to mess around, he's heading over there right now. I need you to get him straight. I'll get you your money later."

He hung up. I still wasn't sure if the bald guy was fucking with me or not, but I got dressed just in case. The doorbell rang; I answered and yeah, there was Kurt, bangs covering his eyes and pretty much looking like shit. He sat down on my couch, I gave him some drugs, he stayed there for a few hours. Sometimes he felt like talking. He'd just read some book about political protests and he was pissed off at it because he didn't think non-violence was the way to go.

"Get a shotgun and just fucking solve the problem, you know?" His eyes were half-closed when he said it.

We talked about music for a little while too. He just rattled off band I didn't know after band I didn't know. Some of the blues guys I'd at least heard the names of, that was it.

"What about you Jimmy?" My name isn't Jimmy. "What are you into?"

My mind went blank. I said something stupid about Led Zeppelin. He didn't answer - he hardly moved, his shoulders just shook a little bit. At first I was worried that he'd fucked up his head and I'd have to get him to a hospital or something, but then I realized he was laughing at me. I wasn't sure if he even knew he was doing it.

I laughed along with him. Why the hell not, I'm a friendly guy, he's a guest in my home, he's a rock star. Nothing wrong with laughing at yourself a little bit.

"Yeah, well. And then there's your stuff right? Everything you guys have done is amazing. I really like it."

He stopped moving. I was worried about him again. Then I saw that he was looking at me. It was the same look my relatives gave me every Thanksgiving when I told them I was still trying to get into the music business after all this time.

He stayed there in my living room for another hour or so getting fucked up, then he left. I tried to call the bald guy back up and see about getting paid, but I just got a voice mail. I kept calling him over the next few days and never had any luck. When I finally got him on the phone I was really pissed off.

"Hey, man." He sounded exhausted, it made me lay off a little bit more than I thought I would.

"Hey. You owe me money."

"Yeah, I know. I know you can't exactly take checks, I'll send somebody over with an envelope."

"I had a lot of trouble getting ahold of you, have you been avoiding me?"

"I've been avoiding everybody. Kurt's lost his fucking mind."

"He's a fucking asshole."

He laughed. "He really is."

"At least he's on his way out. He's twenty-seven now, right? That's when Hendrix bit the dust."

"Yeah, Morrison too."

"Probably worth more money dead. Less hassle anyway." It was supposed to be a joke. There was silence on the other end . I felt a hole open up in my stomach.

"You know, you're a smart kid." He hung up the phone.

And that was it. You know as much as I do about the details. There's any number of people he could've called with a job like that. Yeah, there was a note, so what. Probably cost extra.

A few months later the bald guy finally offered me a job. I took it, I was really good at it, just like I always knew I'd be. I got rich. He never mentioned the conversation we'd had.

I'm sitting here now in my big expensive house, typing on the old-fashioned keyboard I still like to use, listening to the radio on my state of the art sound system. All I have to do is press a button and everything I've written will be available to people all over the world. Some of them will be old like me, but most of them won't, most of them will live forever. The world will get smaller and smaller and smaller as time goes on. They're all going to end up knowing each other really well by the end of things.

Imagine living forever with a prick like that.

I think it worked. I feel better now.

A Black Hole in Chicago

1

I showed up at the diner around nine o'clock. George and Oscar were already there, along with a couple of people I didn't know. Oscar was telling a story. Oscar used to be an EMT, we'd first met when I was still on the force.

"I got called to a convenience store parking lot," Oscar said. "At first I didn't see what the problem was, the call said something about shots fired but they were pretty sketchy about the details. I was worried that maybe things hadn't died down yet, but everything seemed okay. The parking lot was empty except for a giant purple Lincoln. The paint job on this car was beautiful, it practically glowed, it was one of those layered custom things. And when I got closer I saw there was a glass chandelier hanging from the ceiling of the car."

There was a woman in a red coat standing across the street, watching the diner. Watching me, it felt like, but I doubted that was really it. You know how it is, you see somebody attractive, you want to think that they see you too, but I'd been dead for many years at that point and didn't expect the ladies to start checking me out.

"I walked around to the front of the car. The windshield was shattered and there was a guy in the driver's seat with the top of his head just blown off. And the thing was, the guy was a pimp. I mean, he was dressed like a pimp, he was wearing purple fur, he had rings on his fingers, he even had a little custom cup-holder for his fucking gold pimp goblet.

"So of course my partner gets on the horn and tells everybody they need to come down and see this shit. Twenty minutes later that parking lot was full of ambulances..."

She was still there. If she was just gawking she'd have been gone already, it was cold out. She took out a cigarette; she tried to block the wind with her hand, but couldn't get the thing lit.

I slid out of the booth. The guys hardly noticed.

"You can imagine how they freaked out when he started moving again, people weren't used to that yet..."

I left the diner and crossed the street. She saw me coming. There were a couple of different ways this could go; I figured the most likely thing was for her to run away. I wouldn't have blamed her if she had. The smell isn't so bad outdoors, and it's not like I'm missing an eye or anything, but still.

She held her ground, though.

"Need a hand?" I took a box of stick matches out of my pocket.

"Sure," she said, barely getting it out.

I took a step closer and moved over to the left a little bit so that my body was blocking the wind.

"You're welcome to just light it yourself. My fingernails are purple for christ sake, I'm not going to blame you if you want a little personal space."

She actually smiled for a second. Been a long time since I'd pulled off that one.

"No, I'm fine, you can light it."

Worked for me. I took out a match and lit her cigarette. She didn't even flinch. I liked her already.

"You know, if you really want to check out some dead people you're more then welcome to come inside. The place smells like shit but folks are friendly."

"You sure?"

Sure I was sure. She came in and we found her a seat. The conversation slowed down for a moment; George had been about to tell a story but he wasn't sure.

"I don't know if I should tell this one with a lady present…"

She smirked. "I'm no lady. Go right ahead."

He shrugged. A long gouge on the side of his neck closed and reopened. "All right, but don't say I didn't warn you. This was years ago, all right? I was young, that's how long ago this was. I was just moving out of my parents' house and was having trouble finding an apartment I could afford. I finally found a place, but it was two bedrooms. I could afford it if I could find a roommate. So I signed a twelve-month lease and started poking around.

"I finally found a guy. I was running out of time and he seemed to have his head screwed on straight, so I gave him the deal one more time, how much the rent was, how long the lease was. He agreed and we shook hands.

"The very first thing he said after finishing that handshake was 'We need to get some furniture up in this bitch if we're going to get any fucking pussy.'"

The table was silent, including our guest, and for a second I was worried that he'd pissed her off. Then I realized she was trying not to laugh. George saw it too and kept going.

"I lived with this asshole in for a year. Pussy this, pussy that, everything was fucking pussy. Drove me nuts."

She'd started laughing, quietly, she was kind of biting her lip. He went in for the kill.

"He used to be some kind of big deal wrestler in high school. Sometimes he got nostalgic. How did he put it: 'I must be getting ugly. Used to be I could stick my head out of a car going thirty miles an hour and pussy would smack me in the face…'"

The entire table burst out laughing. Oscar held his hand over his right eye to keep it from falling out.

2

It felt nice to explain something to somebody who really knew how to listen. George and Oscar didn't get it - they were polite but sooner or later they just started telling stories again. They talked to each other, I talked to her.

"A finger gets chopped off or one of our lungs rots away, it's not a big deal, everything else keeps on moving like nothing happened. But it doesn't grow back. And everything that used to grow stops, fingernails, hair, anything like that.

"It's the same way in our heads. All the stuff that used to be there pretty much still is, but not much new happens. Me and George and Oscar used to like to tell stories, so we tell stories. Some guys like to argue, you can find a batch of them here any given night yelling at each other. But nobody really learns anything. Things change, it's like they disappeared, there's no transition."

"But all the stuff you're telling me right now, you couldn't have known any of this before you died."

"I used to be a detective. I was a cop for a while and then I was in business for myself. I spent all my time figuring stuff out, it was a routine for me, so I still do it."

"It's a habit."

"Exactly. Like hitting on cute girls."

I was going for another smile there but didn't get it.

"How'd your wife feel about that, cowboy?"

"All right, wait a minute… Look, it wasn't like I followed up on anything, you know? I mean I loved her, I wouldn't do that to her. I just like making dirty jokes."

Her face held that bad-smell look for a bit and then she dropped it.

"Can't fault you for that, I guess. You miss her, though?"

"Would if I could, no doubt about it. But I really can't. It still feels like I saw her just yesterday, you know? Like I've taken a little trip out of town and she's waiting for me back home."

And now she looked sad. She turned her head a little bit, like she was paying attention to George and Oscar and not to me, but really her mind was somewhere else.

I climbed up on top of the table. Either she'd love this or it'd scare the hell out of her.

"Pardon me, everybody. Excuse me, excuse me." Everybody shut up. "We've got a guest joining us from the land of the living tonight, and I think we need to kick things up a notch if we going to prove ourselves worthy of her company.

"You all know this one. Dust in the wind…"

The rest of diner joined in. They sounded like a sclerotic accordion.

"…WE'RE ALL JUST, DUST IN THE WIND!"

We sung the whole song. Everybody knew the words.

3

She was amused, wasn't getting that far-off look anymore. Worked for me. I told her some more cop stories and asked her about herself. She was in college, but she wasn't sure what she wanted to do after she graduated and felt bad about the money. The same crap you always hear from kids in college. I could tell she was going to be fine.

"So why do you think this is happening? People are putting a lot of money into scientists and stuff and they're still coming up empty."

"Beats me. I know there's a lot of churches filling up over it."

"That's what you think? Act of god? Are you religious?"

She said it delicately, like maybe she was going to offend me. I shook my head.

"No, but who knows? There was a guy used to come in here, a preacher, crazy guy. Tried to convince us we were in purgatory. Obviously that's not it, we're in the same old world with you guys. So I don't know. I don't know anything about religion myself, I just get to pick on everybody else."

She looked relieved. "Yeah, me too."

The morning crept up on us. Dead people get tired when there's too much light around. People started clearing out. We went outside and watched the sun come up.

"I guess you're probably going to want to get some rest," she said.

"You got it. It's been nice talking with you though. Come on by anytime."

She had that look on her face again.

"I... Thanks. It was really nice to talk to you for a while."

I was going to ask her what she meant by that when she pulled a gun out of her coat and shot me in the head. Even now I can't remember what she looked like when she did it, what the look on her face was.

Things got weird; the color of the sidewalk smelled like chocolate, the sun on my skin sounded like a bell ringing.

I crawled into an alley and passed out. I don't remember doing it, that's just where I was when I woke up, I got back onto my feet just in time to watch the sun go down. There was shit dribbling out of the hole in my forehead. I grabbed a rag from a dumpster and shoved it in there as far as it would go.

You know the feeling when you hear the name of a song you like on the radio and forget it later, but keep hearing the song? Drives you crazy, and when you finally remember it comes out of nowhere, no rhyme or reason to it at all.

Yeah, it felt like that.

4

He was living on the right side of a duplex. I got his address through an old friend at the department; it was a little after midnight by the time I got to the place.

I banged on the door for about five minutes. His eyes got wide like dinner plates as soon as he saw me. He turned and ran. I went in after him. There was something that looked like a bedroom door on the left and a counter on the right with an oven and a sink behind it, a little kitchen nook. No way out that I could see except the window, and it was closed.

One thing about being dead is that everybody's faster than you are. He jumped up from behind the counter and stabbed me in the chest with a bread knife. My heart beat a couple of times, pumping a brown-red mess through the cut, staining my jacket.

I knocked the knife out of his hand and grabbed him. I pulled him into me, let him get a nice full taste of my mouthwash.

"You know what a black hole is, Markie?"

He didn't answer, didn't know.

"It's what guys like me call the last five minutes or so before we got killed. We don't usually remember it, which means we aren't always sure how exactly we died. Except you were the last person I was with right before I died, and you're a fucking asshole, so I'm thinking you fucking shot me. Does that sound right to you?"

He nodded his head yes, frantically.

"Your reason or somebody else's?"

He didn't want to answer. I squeezed his forearm and exhaled.

"Bob Reely," he said. "He paid for it…"

I recognized the name. His wife had hired me to take some pictures. They were getting divorced, he had money. It doesn't always have to be complicated.

"You wouldn't happen to have an address for Mr. Reely?"

5

I tied Markie to a chair in his kitchen with a bunch of rope I found under his sink and patched up my chest with a giant band-aid from his medicine cabinet. I didn't have any evidence except his word and you have no idea how fucking complicated it is for somebody in my situation to testify in court. Maybe I'd find some evidence at Bob's place, maybe I wouldn't find anything and that skinny little bastard would get loose and try to lay down an assault charge on me. I didn't give a fuck. I was pretty pissed off by now.

Bob's house was nicer then Markie's. When I got there the door was open, actually swinging open, pushed and pulled by the wind coming in and out of the breezeway. I went inside.

I met him in his living room. He was waiting for me, looking right at me as I walked inside, sitting in an easy chair. He was a smooth-skinned little fat man - he had no hair left and was wearing a bathrobe. He was trying not to look scared and doing a decent job of it.

"Well, this is a riot, Max," he said. "I just didn't think this was ever gonna happen. I hope your little girl didn't cry too much at your funeral."

I took a step forward. Then some asshole hit me in the back of the head with a sledgehammer.

I fell over. It took me a second to realize I was still moving. I reached around to where I'd gotten hit, felt my fingertips sink into my skull like it was a rotten melon. The hammer came down again and missed me, made a nice hole in the floor.

I got up and turned around. Markie was trying to lift the hammer for another swing. He had nice red burn marks on his arms where I'd tied him.

That was when I really got angry.

6

Most of what you hear about people like me is bullshit. Urban legends, you know. Even things that are real get blown out of proportion. Having said that, it's a really bad idea to upset me, and there wasn't much left of Bob and Markie to get back up by the time I was finished.

There was blood all over my clothes, so I took some stuff from Bob's closet and changed. I traded the rag in my head for a washcloth with his initials monogrammed on it and went back into the living room.

I made a few more phone calls, old friends, family. All it really takes to find somebody is persistence, doesn't matter who you are. She lived in an apartment building. I was tired by the time I got there, it was daytime.

I rang her buzzer.

"I was hoping I could talk to you for a minute," I said. "I'm not mad or anything, I just wanted to talk to you."

She buzzed me in and I slowly climbed the stairs. I knocked on her door, but held it shut when she tried to open it.

"I don't look so hot," I said. "You might not want to look at me. We can just talk through the door if you want."

She opened the door. Tough kid.

"I thought you didn't remember."

I shrugged. "I've been getting a lot in the way of head trauma lately, that's probably got something to do with it."

She looked like maybe she was going to cry, but she held it back. I went into the apartment and gave her a hug. It didn't occur to me that maybe she wouldn't want to get hugged by a corpse. Old habits. She hugged me right back, though.

"I'm sorry," she said, and now she was crying.

"You worry too much," I said. "Even if you had put me down it's not like I would've minded. I'm dead, kiddo. Shit, you can shoot me again now if you really want to. Makes no difference to me."

She put her head on my shoulder. "I thought I was doing you a favor."

"Not really. But it was a nice thought. Here, let me take a look at you." I held her at arm's distance.

We went inside and talked for a while. She told me more about school, what kinds of stuff she'd been up to, how her mom had been. By the end of it I was exhausted.

"Look," I said. "You can come by and visit again if you feel like it, but I can't guarantee that I'll recognize you."

"I don't think I will," she said. "It was probably a bad idea to come by in the first place."

"Don't know if I'd say that. Last time I saw you, you were playing soccer on a park district team. Kind of nice to see how you turned out."

She smiled, I was glad to be able to do that one more time. "All right?"

"Yeah. But you picked that gun out to match your purse, get something real if you're going to be shooting people, okay?"

She laughed, even better. I gave her a hug.

"Love you, Dad."

"Love you too."

And I left.

Quiet

1

Sleepy drove back to his building and took the elevator to the third floor. He heard Doc yelling as the doors slid open and saw a naked man with rope burns all over his body sprint past. Sleepy dropped the Chinese food and tackled him, got him on his back and hit him in the face. He kept squirming; there was blood streaming down his nose, staining his teeth and his mustache. Sleepy hit him again. The blow connected with the side of the naked man's head and he stopped moving.

Sleepy stood up, grabbed the naked man's ankles, and dragged him towards the apartment. A pretty older woman in a bathrobe poked out her head just as they got him through the doorway.

"You didn't see shit, ma'am!" Doc shouted, and they closed the door. There were still two take-out boxes lying on the ground near the elevator.

There had been seven of them originally, but the only orders they'd gotten were calls home for guys on the team, nothing about what they were supposed to do with the target. It had been down to Sleepy and Doc for nearly two weeks. The target's name was Harry Nelson. They called him Harry when they had to call him something. Usually you called the target by their last name but Harry had stayed Harry for some reason.

They had nothing they were supposed to do except babysit the fax machine. It was like waiting for a girl to call you back.

"You've got good reflexes," Doc said.

He finished up, took a step back, and wiped the sweat from his forehead.

"Don't know how he got out. Fucking Houdini, this guy."

Sleepy was sitting on the couch. If they'd lost the target he'd have been dead, even if it hadn't been his thought. Close call, but Sleepy didn't feel it, he felt good. It was like a gap had opened up in his chest and given everything room to stretch out. Also, he had an erection, something that had been happening at odd times lately and which he tried hard not to think about too much.

Doc dipped into the kitchen and came back with a long carving fork. He waved its prongs slowly in front of the naked man's face.

"Teach you to run on me, motherfucker."

He'd been hitting the prisoner pretty hard over the last few days, beating him up, messing with his food, fucking with his head in different ways. Nothing that cut the skin, though.

"We need him in one piece," Sleepy said, not sure if he was overstepping his bounds. Doc wasn't the type to pull rank often, but he was technically still in charge.

"He'll stay in one piece." He smirked and lowered the point of the fork, gently pressed it against the skin underneath the naked man's left nipple.

Sleepy stared at the man's chest, then snapped out of it. "Shit…" He turned his head away and closed his eyes. "I'm gonna go watch TV."

"You're welcome to stay," Doc said, but Sleepy went into the kitchen.

The television was sitting on the table on the opposite side of the room from the sink. Reception was bad; they didn't have cable, it was a security thing. The only show that stayed in tune was about a crime lab that used high-tech tools to catch serial killers.

The fax machine came to life, shaking the table as the machinery buzzed and the gears turned. Sleepy read the new orders as they came through. He read them again when they were done printing, then again, then one more time.

He opened a drawer and lifted up the Tupperware that contained the cutlery. Underneath was a stack of old order sheets. They were supposed to destroy them, but nobody wanted to be the guy who fucked up because he forgot something and didn't have any way to double check.

Sleepy dug through the pile until he found what he wanted, put it down on the counter next to the new orders, and read them both.

They were fucked.

3

He had to bang on the door for more than five minutes before Doc opened it a crack and stuck his head through. He was holding the fork. There was blood on the tip of one of the prongs.

"What?"

"The orders. I think we're in deep shit."

Doc looked past Sleepy, over at the fax machine, and put on his business face.

"Give me a second, all right?"

He closed the door. Sleepy could hear him talking.

"I'm going to give you a little break now, but I'm going to leave this here to give you something to think about. See you in a few minutes."

He returned to the kitchen without the fork.

"What's up?"

Sleepy showed him the new fax:

SORRY FOR THE WAIT, BOYS. CONTINUE TO DETAIN HARRY NEILSON. BURN AFTER READING.

"Probably just a typo," Doc said. He didn't look worried.

"No shit, which fucking one?"

"Keep your voice down, we got neighbors." He was still staring in the direction of the orders, but not at them. Sleepy paced back and forth across the kitchen, letting Doc talk. "Either Nelson is the bad guy and the first message had the mistake or Neilson is the bad guy and the second message had the mistake. It's a coin flip."

"It's a fuckup. As soon as somebody realizes they made a mistake the whole operation is gonna get cleaned."

"Relax, relax." Doc crumpled the old orders into a ball and turned on the garbage disposal. "The new orders are asking for a Neilson. We'll make sure we have a Nelson for them."

"You mean a Neilson."

"Yeah, that's what I mean." Doc laughed. "See, this is the whole problem with grabbing white people. If we got an Abdel mixed up with a Abdullah nobody would care. I mean shit, we're supposed to be fighting fucking terrorism."

Sleepy just stared at him.

"All right, sorry, not funny. Anyway, we got to make sure that the guy we have in there is a Neilson. We have to wash him out like a pair of muddy jeans. Low protein diet in a pitch black room, the whole nine yards."

"You know how to do all that?"

"Sure. I'm going to need help, though."

"No. No way."

"Come on. It's not like you're not an asshole. We're all assholes here. You don't mind hurting people."

"Not like that."

"So what you're saying is, you don't want to grab this guy's balls and watch the look in his eyes when he goes from not believing what's happening to not knowing what's going to happen next. You don't want to make him cry, you don't want to make him beg. That's not you."

Sleepy didn't answer, he just stood there.

"I'll tell you what," Doc continued. "There's no reason to argue until we're sure of the situation. How about we just go over in the next room and ask our subject how his last name is spelled in a way that we're sure he'll answer? You're going to want to hear what he has to say firsthand, right? Just to make sure?"

Doc opened the door.

The naked man was on the floor. His chair was tipped over. He was still tied to it but he'd gotten one of his arms free and he'd been able to drag himself over to where Doc had left the fork. He'd cut his own throat.

Sleepy and Doc were silent. Doc approached the body.

"Guy had a real talent for slipping out of a rope," he finally said.

He crouched down, took a closer look. "Fuckin' Houdini, this guy."

4

They left the corpse in the apartment and drove around for a while. They found someone; he was wearing a flannel shirt and he was by himself. Just walking down the street at four o'clock in the morning. They stopped the car.

"Is there something I could help you guys with…"

Sleepy punched him in the throat. He gagged and fell forward. Doc grabbed his neck and choked him until he was unconscious. They carried him over to the car and threw him in the trunk.

They gagged him, wrapped some bungee cords around his wrists and ankles, and slammed the trunk shut.

5

They got further orders three weeks later. They still had to sit tight for a few more days, but they could come home after that. They had Harry locked in the closet. He knew what his name was; it hadn't taken long.

Their last night at the apartment there was a thunderstorm and the TV didn't work. They played Scrabble. Sleepy had a Q and a bunch of vowels. He knew there was a place for them somewhere, but couldn't quite make them fit.

"I'm glad everything worked out," Doc said. "You have a real touch, you know that?"

Sleepy didn't say anything.

"It's nothing to be afraid of."

Sleepy looked away from the board.

"Is it normal?"

"Beats me," Doc said. "But they never have trouble finding people."

Sleepy dumped his tiles into the bag and got seven new ones.

"Your move," he said quietly.

Doc put his letters down right away.

"My advice would be to enjoy it," he said. "While it's something fresh. Before it's just a job."

Ducks

The summer of my junior year in high school I had a job at the Open Window retirement community going around to the residents' apartments doing odd jobs. My boss was a guy named Dr. Amal. He'd hired me because a few of the residents suddenly decided they hated all the nursing staff; he thought it'd blow over, but in the meantime he thought it might be a good idea to have a fresh face up there.

It wasn't a hard job, I did laundry and moved boxes, whatever the residents wanted. The only one I ever felt like I had a real relationship with was a Jewish widow named Greta. Greta set herself apart in a lot of ways. She never wanted to talk about her life. There were no pictures of her family in her apartment. I never found out what jobs she'd held or where she'd grown up, and she seemed to get along better with the staff then with any of her neighbors. She and Dr. Amal had a little routine going - every time he came by to check on her she'd pretend to be freaked out that her "ancient enemy" had broken into her home and they'd spend five or ten minutes making jokes about whatever terrible things were going on in the Middle East that month.

One day I was walking down the hall towards Greta's apartment when I saw a guy my own age walking in the opposite direction. He was about twice my size, and older than me. He wore black pants and had a leather strap with metal studs sticking out of it wrapped around his left wrist. His face was flat and doughy, expressionless.

When I came to Greta's door it was already open. I went inside. Greta was leaning back in her chair.

"Greta?"

She opened her eyes. "It is time for you to stop by isn't it…"

"Greta, did somebody just visit you?"

"My punk of a grandson. Does he look as ugly as he sounds?"

I cleared my throat. "He failed to take after you."

"You're a charmer. Show some mercy and help me up."

I took her by the hand and got her out of the chair. As she rose, I noticed a grocery bag full of white bread next to the chair, a dozen loaves in a neat stack. Greta went through a lot of bread.

"Ducks hungry yesterday, Greta?"

"They got babies, they got to eat something."

There were no ducks anywhere around Open Window. I suspected that she'd been feeding geese, which tended to hang out in the rock garden on the ground near the highway, but whenever I brought it up she insisted she could hear the difference and if I pressed the issue she suggested that maybe the ducks only came out at night.

"I didn't know they let you guys hit the town at night."

"It's a stupid rule. I sneak out."

"Wild and crazy."

"I feed birds. Aren't you supposed to be working or something?"

I spent a few minutes dusting off some shelves before she shoved a book in my hand. I read to her for about an hour and a half.

I didn't see her again until the following week. She didn't come to her door when I knocked, and when I went into her room, she had her chair turned towards the window. She was watching the lunch-hour traffic with a sad look in her eyes. I'd never seen her like this.

"Greta?"

She sighed without turning away from the window. "My grandson stopped by again this morning."

"He did?"

"You bet he did. He let it slip that he thought he was getting in the will somehow and we ended up yelling at each other for about half an hour."

I glanced back at the front door to her apartment. "Do you want me to talk to the front desk, keep him from coming up here?"

"He's my grandson. I'm not going to kick him out. Shit, I've been putting up with rotten kids for so long." She sighed again. "Maybe you could skip the housework today and just read me something."

So I read her poetry until my shift was over.

When I went to work the next morning there were two cops standing in front of the entrance to Greta's building. Dr. Amal came jogging through the doors, grabbed my arm, and escorted me around the corner. Greta'd gotten hurt and her entire extended family was camped out in the lobby looking for someone to blame. He wanted me to go home and stay there until things were sorted out. That was it, he didn't have time to get into the details, he went back inside as soon as he was sure I was leaving.

I went back to the fence behind the building where I'd locked my bike. My bike lock was a thick chain with a giant padlock on the end of it. I'd been pretty sure it would be impossible to pry off, but when I got back it was gone.

I went home and tried not to worry, killed the day reading and playing video games. I didn't start thinking about it again until after dinner. I was trying to figure out who would want to steal my bike lock but not my bike. Once I started thinking about that I started wondering how my bike got stolen when I only was only away from it for a few minutes.

Because somebody was waiting for an opportunity. And Greta snuck out by herself at night. The only phone number I had for Open Window was Dr. Amal's office and nobody was there. I left the house and got on my bike.

I ditched my bike by the front gate and made my way towards the rock garden. The only light came from the streetlights shining through the slots of the fence by the highway. I saw Greta. She was holding a plastic grocery bag in her right hand and a cane in her left. She was walking towards a drainage pipe near the edge of the park. I heard a noise coming from inside of it. Greta was right, it sounded more like a goose then a duck, but it didn't sound much like a goose either. I wasn't sure what it was.

Greta took a piece of bread and threw it down near the pipe. I saw something move very quickly near the entrance. The bread was gone.

Something moved in my peripheral vision. I turned my head back at the bushes surrounding one of the main buildings and saw Greta's grandson. He was holding my bike lock. He didn't seem to see me. He moved towards Greta and lifted the chain up over his head.

I ran up, grabbed him from behind, and pulled him backwards. Greta turned around.

"Is somebody there?"

Her grandson hit me in the side of the head with the chain before I could say anything and I fell down. He lifted the chain again.

It moved incredibly quickly. Before I knew what was going on, while I was still dizzy, it crawled out of the pipe and leaped up into the air. It landed behind Greta's grandson and wrapped an enormous pale hand around his shoulder.

In the second it took for me to clear my head it was joined by four more, another big one and three children. They were naked and hairless, with soft pink eyes and skin so pale you could see the veins underneath even in the darkness. They weren't human, but their great-grandparents might have been. They had tiny round heads, like a newborn, and skinny, elongated necks. They swarmed around Greta's grandson, wrapped a hand around his mouth before he could cry out, dragged him away headfirst into the drainage tunnel, and re-emerged a moment later without him.

One of the small ones got down on her knees and inhaled sharply. With visible effort, she pushed the air back through her throat. There it was, that noise. They all started doing it, squawking and munching on the bread as she threw it down to them.

Greta smiled, relieved.

"There you all are... I was worried about you... there you are, there you are..."

They glanced in my direction every so often, like maybe they were afraid I was going to steal their food, but they didn't bother me. I watched them for a minute, not sure what to say. Then I ran back to my bike and rode home as fast as I could.

Dr. Amal called me a couple of days later. Greta finally admitted that her grandson had hit her, she'd refused to talk about it before. He had a criminal record and had apparently blown town without telling anybody where he was going, so I was in the clear no matter what kind of noise the rest of Greta's family made. I could come back to work.

I didn't know what I was expecting when I went back to Greta's room, but I still managed to be surprised. Everything was just like it'd been, like nothing had happened. Greta was sitting in her chair waiting for me.

"Hey kid."

"Greta…"

She waved her hand at me. She had some stitches over her eye, I hadn't seen them before. "It's nothing. Don't even talk about it. It's nothing."

She pointed at some shelves she wanted me to dust and waited until I got to work before she said anything else.

"It's always been like this. You've just got to get that through your head so you won't worry about me any more. I'm used to taking care of things."

"You're talking about your family."

"Yeah, family."

I finished dusting.

"You want me to read you anything?"

"Not yet, I got more real work for you. There's some stuff in the fridge. Could you dump it in the sink and run some water over it for me please?"

I went into the kitchen and opened her fridge. There was a giant stack of T-bone steaks sitting on the bottom shelf.

"Just get them thawed out."

"What are these for, Greta?"

"They're for the ducks."

"I thought the ducks ate bread, Greta."

I looked over at her. She was still sitting in her chair. If anything, she seemed more comfortable than she had before.

"They like this better now."

32

Dinosaurs

1

I was standing on the roof of a building downtown. It was a beautiful day. She hadn't shown up yet. I stretched out and started talking to myself.

"So how's it going?"

I sat down and dangled my feet over the edge.

"I wonder why they don't try to eat each other?"

The air smelled like sulfur for a moment before the wind blew it away and there she was, sitting next to me. We looked down at the street together and watched the dinosaurs. A triceratops and a tyrannosaurus were staring peacefully at one another from opposite sides of a crashed helicopter.

"It's because they're dead. They don't get angry or hungry anymore. The big guy had been keeping them in heaven, but after he called all the people back he needed space."

"That doesn't make any sense. If God needed room for something He'd just make more room. It's not like He's running a warehouse."

She shrugged and smiled, looking about like you'd expect the devil to look but warm too, like a big sister, not like she was going to tear my heart out or anything. She reminded me of my ex-wife, actually.

"Yeah, maybe. Come on, let's play."

So we played tennis. She offered me a drink of water after we were done but I turned her down. She smiled, that same big-sister smile.

"You can drink the water. I wouldn't mess with you like that, honest."

I smiled back. "Promise me on a stack of Bibles and maybe I'll believe you."

She didn't laugh but I could tell she thought it was funny. We played one more game and she disappeared. She didn't even say goodbye - her last serve landed on the wrong side of the line and she vanished.

2

I still had a few hours to kill before the sun set, so I rode my bike around until my legs hurt; when I finally got tired I went to the Art Institute, and when that got boring I went to the library. When the sun began to set I left the library and headed over to a bookstore downtown called Adult World.

I headed back to the hotel to get some sleep. I'd always been a night person, but not any more. Once, I'd set myself up in my room with some books and a pot of coffee and just refused to go to sleep until the sun came up, but it didn't work out too well. By morning I was exhausted, and I knew if I went to bed it would be dark again by the time I woke up, and morning by the time I wanted to go back to sleep. So I'd set a nine o'clock curfew and I'd held to it ever since.

The night after my last game of tennis I slept like a baby. When I got up again and looked out the window, the dinosaurs were gone.

3

I went to the grocery store and grabbed a can of clam chowder off the shelf, then I rode to a restaurant down the street where the stove still worked, heated up the chowder, and sat down in the VIP room with an old newspaper. When I was done eating I left the dishes where they were and went over to a bowling alley a few blocks away. None of the equipment was still running, but I'd tied a skateboard to the score machine with a rope so that I could ride it back and forth to retrieve my ball and set up the pins by hand after each roll. I think I got a bigger kick out of the whole apparatus than from actually bowling, and I knew I'd get bored with it sooner or later. That wasn't a big deal, I'd just come up with something else to do. There was always something. So I bowled for a while, and then I felt like working on my sculpture.

My sculpture was a work in progress sitting in the middle of an intersection a block or so from the lake. I thought it was funny to have it there; I could imagine the horns honking in all four directions leading from it, a giant traffic jam just waiting for this big hulking thing to get out of the way.

I was sifting through the scrap pile trying to figure out what I wanted to use next when I heard the devil's voice behind me.

"You're really freaked out, aren't you?"

I turned around. It was the first time in weeks she'd come to talk to me except to play tennis.

"By what?"

"The dinosaurs going away."

"I don't care."

"Bullshit. You've hardly blinked all morning. You're tense."

"Maybe I just felt like getting some stuff done."

I turned around and threw a car bumper onto the scrap pile. The sculpture was about ten feet tall and getting taller the more I added to it. The height was the important thing. I knew I was no kind of artist, but I figured a giant metal sculpture smack-dab in the middle of a major intersection in downtown Chicago was kind of cool just for being what it was.

I realized that I was sweating.

"All right," I said. "I miss the fucking dinosaurs. You got to get in a routine when you're living like this, and having something big like that change for no reason kind of threw me off."

"You're not going crazy, are you?"

I didn't answer her.

"Well, I hope not. Look, I came here to tell you that somebody's coming. Her name is Danielle Wyner. She's been around for a while, but she stayed away from downtown because of the dinosaurs."

She lost me at somebody. It took me a moment to figure out what she was talking about.

"You don't look all that excited about this. Don't you think you could use some company?"

I turned my attention back to the car bumper. It was pretty dinged up, but had a lot of chrome left on it. I decided to use it, and tried to figure out how I was going to move it to the 'use' pile without cutting up my fingers.

The devil shrugged.

"She'll be here in a few days. You might want to shave."

I didn't look up until I was sure she was gone.

4

I didn't shave, but for the first time in months, I felt self-conscious about it. I moved my bedroom to the corner suite on the second story of the hotel, and I got in the habit of looking out the window with binoculars every morning.

Four days later I saw her. She was riding a motorcycle down Michigan Avenue; I could see a couple of inches of red hair poking out from under her helmet and a hunting rifle slung over her shoulder with a dark green canvas strap. She parked the motorcycle in front of a meter, hung her helmet from one of the handlebars, and looked around for a moment. Then she walked towards my hotel.

I jumped away from the window and tried to figure out how the hell she knew I was here; when I crawled back and peeked down at the sidewalk I saw a garbage can next to the front door of the hotel, filled to overflowing with pop cans I'd emptied over the past few months. I felt like an idiot. I locked the door to my room and slid the chain in place but I changed my mind immediately. I couldn't just let her wander around the building doing whatever she wanted, I had to keep track of her.

I decided to check the kitchen first. I got in the elevator, went back down to the lobby, and walked through the restaurant. I pushed through the swing doors and peeked around the corner. She was sitting at the manager's desk, eating a sandwich. There was a pile of random paper on the floor next to her and her gun was slung casually over the back of her chair like it was a coat.

I pulled myself back. My hand brushed up against something, and I whirled around just in time to see a serving tray hit the ground and shatter into a million pieces. When I looked back up she was standing in front of me.

"You don't have to worry about the gun," she said quietly. "I only brought it in case the monsters came back."

She wasn't lying - she'd left the gun by the desk. "Yeah, that's good." It was a stupid thing to say. I'd have felt more embarrassed if she didn't already seem to be embarrassed herself.

I found myself turning away from her, looking for something else to focus on. I saw a container of tuna salad on the counter that she'd used in her sandwich. I kept the tuna salad behind a bunch of other stuff, which meant that I knew she'd had to push some stuff out of the way to get what she wanted.

"I kind of had things arranged here. I gathered everything together..."

"This is a huge city, you can't just call dibs on everything."

"No, I didn't mean that at all... Look, I'm not hoarding or anything. I'd just appreciate it if you could keep everything straight. Leave things how you found them. I'd really appreciate it."

She still looked skeptical; I kept talking.

"Look, I know it's silly, it's just how I've been keeping my head straight. Keeping everything in order."

She didn't say anything for a moment, just kind of looked me over, and when she spoke again I was sure she felt sorry for me. "Sure. You don't have to worry."

And that was it. It was amazing how little we had to say to each other. I went back up to my room, and she went back to eating her sandwich. About twenty minutes later I saw her through my window as she walked back to her motorcycle.

I ran into her once or twice a day over the course of the next few weeks. None of our conversations lasted any longer then our introduction in the kitchen. Some part of me kind of hoped that she'd ask me for advice, directions or something, but she never did. Still though, things got better. We began to nod when we passed on the street. Eventually we started saying hello.

One time I saw her walking towards me on the opposite side of the street. I waved to her; she waved back and shouted at me.

"Good morning!"

I shouted back.

"Morning! What do you have there?"

"Some books from the library. I marked where they all came from, so I won't put them back in the wrong place."

It took me a second to realize she was making fun of me. She was smiling, though, and I found that I was too, in spite of myself.

"Thanks. Thanks a lot."

"No problem. Have a good day."

"You too."

We walked past each other.

I worked on my sculpture all morning. It was more then twenty feet tall now - I'd had to build scaffolding all around it so I could climb to the top. I glanced at my watch. It was past lunch; I put my stuff down and wiped the sweat off my forehead. When I opened my eyes the devil was standing in front of me.

"How's the tower coming along?"

I looked up. "I hadn't really thought of it that way."

"How's Danielle?"

"You might get a better answer if you asked her, but she seems all right."

"So why aren't you with her?"

Lunch, I reminded myself. I ducked under the guardrail and climbed back down to the street. The devil was waiting for me when my feet touched the sidewalk.

"You still haven't answered my question."

"I don't know, I think that we'd both rather be alone most of the time. "

"You've been alone already."

"So what? Things are nice how they are."

"Doesn't mean things couldn't be better. Why don't you try talking to her a little more often?"

"You know, I was never very religious, but I'm pretty sure that if the devil shows up in person and tells you to do something you probably shouldn't do it."

She disappeared.

I stopped work on the sculpture at five o'clock and rode down to the bookstore. I was lying on the back counter with my pants down around my ankles when the devil reappeared.

"I thought I'd try talking to you sometime when you wouldn't be so smug."

I flailed around trying to cover myself and fell flat on my ass onto the floor behind the cash register. I zipped my fly and stood up.

"When you poke your head outside you'll see a cloud of smoke from a neighborhood that just got torched by a motorcycle gang called the Vipers. They've cruised by Chicago a few times but they always kept a distance because of the dinosaurs. Mostly they just grab whatever they want, beat on the heads of anybody they find and move on, but they haven't made it to a town this nice yet that wasn't already taken, so they might be sticking around."

"Did you do this?"

She was gone before the words were even out of my mouth. I stopped for a second to tuck in my shirt and ran out of the store.

The sun was setting, but the smoke was there, just like she said, a thin trickle rising above the skyline. I was trying to think of a list of places Danielle might be when I heard her voice behind me.

"Did she talk to you too?"

She was only ten feet away, closer then she'd been in days.

"Who?" I said.

"The devil," she answered.

6

I took her to an office building down the street. The elevator doors were open and the crowbar was where I'd left it under the control panel last year; I picked it up, stuck the sharp end of it into the side of the panel, and tore it off, littering the floor with screws and little pieces of plastic.

We stepped into the elevator; I pressed a button and the doors closed behind us.

"What was that for?"

"I ripped off the panels on all the other floors already except for the top, so nobody can call the elevator back down."

"Doesn't this building have stairs?"

"Yeah, two stairwells. I chained and boarded up all the fire doors and sealed the doors on the top with concrete."

"What happens if somebody sets fire to the building?"

I hadn't thought of that. The doors opened. "Then I guess we're screwed. Come on, let me show you around."

The office was a huge open space, gray walls and dark blue carpeting. There were stacks of boxes, soup, bowls, cups, a microwave to use for as long as the electricity still ran and a propane stove with plenty of spare tanks. I also had some books and a TV set with a DVD player, and a portable generator with a few tanks of gas.

Danielle walked over to the telescope.

"There. Look at that."

I leaned down and put my eye up to the glass. I saw another column of smoke rising up into the air, thicker and large, closer.

Danielle started pacing back and forth. I watched her for a while, then I took a nap. I checked my watch when I woke up again. It was two o'clock in the afternoon, but it was already getting dark.

She was looking out the window, holding her rifle. I got up and went over to her.

"Any more fires?" I asked her.

"No," she whispered.

The sun was hidden behind a slowly growing mass of clouds. An hour later the windows were like black sheets.

Hailstones rattled the windows. The sound was like somebody tapping their fingernails on the glass. We'd decided that leaving the office lights on was too risky, so we were sitting on the floor with a mosquito lantern between us.

"Have you ever seen weather like this?" Danielle asked.

I shook my head no. She leaned back on her hands, moving out of the light so that all I could see was her knees, two worn spots on the jeans she was wearing.

"What did you first think when everybody disappeared?"

I shrugged. "I had a crazy aunt who talked about that all the time, how all the good people were going to get called up to heaven. But I had my doubts about that when I saw that there wasn't anybody else around. I mean, I can't be the worst person in the whole city, right?"

We were quiet for a moment, then I asked her a question.

"How many times have you seen the devil?"

"Only twice, once to tell me that the monsters weren't in the city anymore and again to tell me about the gang."

"How did you know she was the devil?"

"First time she visited she told me. When I told her I didn't believe her she turned a parking garage into sand."

The noise outside had been going on for so long that we didn't really hear it anymore; the darkness stretched on for a few more hours, and the hailstones kept falling. Eventually boredom won out over caution and we turned the lights back on. We watched a couple of movies; we tried to talk about what things were like before the world stopped but we weren't able to find anything that either of us still cared about. We were getting tired, so we took turns sleeping.

I was in the middle of a dream when a bright light woke me up. I heard thunder and looked out the window. There was lightning everywhere, falling from the sky like raindrops, tearing giant chunks out of the buildings before our eyes.

Suddenly the office lights went out. Danielle said something, but the thunder drowned out her voice. Everything stopped, and we were engulfed in darkness. For a moment I thought I was dead.

"Danielle?"

"Yeah?"

I dropped down to the carpet and crawled towards the sound of her voice. We butted heads.

"Ouch."

"Shit."

"Do you know where the lamp is?"

"Somewhere over there."

"Where the hell is that?"

Our hands found each other.

"I have no idea. We'd better stay here."

We stayed there in the middle of the floor until we fell asleep. When I woke up, the sky was blue again.

I walked over to the window and looked down, and saw a brontosaurus walk by.

8

The devil came back to me a couple of weeks later. Danielle had moved into my hotel room and it had long since become our room, our kitchen, our hotel. We'd had sex for the first time last night, and compared to everything else that had been going on it honestly wasn't that big a deal.

She appeared in front of me one morning while I was walking to the library.

"I just wanted to let you know that things aren't going to be getting crazy for a while. The electricity and the heat and everything will work and the dinosaurs will stay where they are, so nobody will come by and bother you. You'll be safe."

"What about that gang?"

"There wasn't any gang. I started the fires myself."

"Why?"

"Because I thought it'd be easier than destroying every piece of pornography in the city of Chicago."

I pushed past her and kept walking. I could hear her footsteps right behind me.

"That's fucking great."

"What are you so upset about?"

"I don't like getting bounced around like a ball on a pool table. And I still don't know why it had to be me."

"It's not a bad thing. You've been picked. The big guy used to do it all the time when he was in charge. You want to go play tennis?"

I was going to yell at her some more but when I turned around she'd disappeared.

9

I didn't come back up to the tennis court for a couple of years, but when I did she was waiting for me.

"What made you show up?"

I shrugged. "I guess I couldn't think of anything better to do today."

I threw the ball back to her and she caught it.

"How's the missus?" she said.

"She thinks I'm out looking for food."

"Sounds like your last marriage. How're the kids?"

"There aren't any kids."

She smiled at me. "You ought to have some."

I imagined coming home to find a pillar of salt where my condom stash used to be. The devil made her serve.

Lake Sympathy

1

It was traveling, and suddenly it was alone. It didn't know if it had made a wrong turn, if the others had left it behind accidentally or on purpose.

It settled on the bottom of a small body of water. There were living things elsewhere on the planet but it didn't mind, they were like soft television static, helping it sleep. It sent out a signal to keep them from getting too close. Thoughts were nothing, electricity passing through tissue, simple to see or alter or extinguish.

One of them approached, despite the signal. Two, it realized, looking more carefully. One of them was an infant.

The other one rose up and nearly disappeared, burnt and crackled and flared.

2

Caroline waited until midnight. Her sister was fast asleep by now and it was dark in the house. She went into Thomas's room, wrapped him in a blanket, and picked him up.

"There you are, there you are…" He didn't make a sound. She stopped by the kitchen for a bread knife and left the house.

The roads took longer than they had to; there were lots of long curves, scenic routes for summer people. At night there were no lights, no buildings, no windows. Trees and stars.

She skidded to a stop, leaned the bike against a road sign and took the baby out of the basket. She went into the woods. The darkness didn't bother her, she knew the way. On the other side of the forest was a cliff that faced the lake. There were weeds growing along the edge; in the middle was an indentation filled with white sand.

She remembered the words from Bob's book, whispered them under her breath, over and over again. She pictured a tomato on a cutting board and held that picture in her mind as she pulled the edge of the knife across the baby's throat.

Warm blood dripped from her fingers. She kept her eyes closed. The tomato was gone now, and she didn't have anything to replace it with, so she focused on the dark. She liked to do that sometimes, to just go into a closet and close the door.

She heard a string of loud noises, like a row of firecrackers hitting a sidewalk but much, much louder, so loud the earth seemed to shake. She remembered what Bob had said about this. It was hard to understand what he was saying most of the time, he mumbled and used big words, but sometimes after they'd fucked he'd get into a weird mood and speak more clearly.

"They live beyond the stars, far outside anything we could see, so far that distance itself doesn't even describe it, but when they do come they'll cross that distance in an instant…"

She opened her eyes and for a moment she saw it, what she'd seen every night in her dreams for as long as she could remember, acres of teeth and boiling skin and eyes of every color, a hammer striking the back of her skull.

And then it was gone. Relief swept through her body. In its place, standing naked on the edge of the cliff, was Bob.

She looked again, more carefully. His face was wrong, the details of his body were glossed over. It wasn't Bob, it was how she'd imagined him, the picture in her head.

She fell to her knees and started chanting again but was interrupted.

"No."

The image spoke.

"I don't want you to serve me. There is nothing you have that I want."

And that was it. And in all the corners of Caroline's mind, every twist and turn, there was nowhere she could convince herself that it had said anything but the truth.

She looked down at her nephew's body.

"Oh, god…"

She stood up. The soles of her shoes slid further into the sand.

"I didn't… I wasn't supposed to be, I mean… I stole the book from Bob, I don't know if you know him…" That was stupid, it didn't care about anything like that. "I stole the book, he was going to do it but I stole the book …"

She grabbed her head, and started making strange noises, crying and breathing quickly.

"No, no…"

She turned and ran, slipping and falling twice before she climbed out and disappeared into the trees.

She came back a few minutes later.

"You came, you heard me. You could have ignored me but you didn't.

"You're real. They say I don't know what's real and what isn't but you're real.

"I'll come back."

3

She stayed away for two years.

"You're still there… I guess it hasn't been that long for you.

"I'm just going to talk to you. Bob would talk a lot about the right and wrong way to say things but I'm not going to do that. If you're going to eat me or something go ahead and eat me. The way Bob talked, I sometimes think that's what he wanted for himself, like that was the best thing he could think of.

"I didn't do anything to Bob. He was always acting like people were out to get him. He was only in town for a couple of months, he disappeared after I stole the book.

"So maybe it was him that was supposed to talk to you, but you've got me instead. At least for a little while, I don't think I'm going to come back here again. I don't really have any place to stay. My sister always knew… what happened, the cops couldn't prove anything but she always knew, she kicked me out of the house right away. I had a couple of friends and I kind of went back and forth between their places. Guys, you know.

"I don't do that so much now. People don't like me around, they don't even let me go to church. It's only a matter of time before they try and lock me up.

"So I'm leaving town. I just need a car and some money. I've had a couple of jobs, I'm saving up. I'm going to be gone soon. I just wanted to check up on you one more time."

She turned away, then back again. It didn't look like Bob anymore, it didn't really look like anything.

"I remember what you told me before, but do you maybe know somewhere I could go? Someplace people don't know about?"

No answer.

"Well, all right then," Caroline said. "All right. Goodbye."

4

Seven years later. She came back during the day. There was nothing there, just water as far as she could see. She was crying. She grabbed her stomach with both hands.

"Please come back. Get rid of it. Make it go away. Please."

Nothing. Not city nothing, middle of nowhere nothing. Silence that seemed to press against her from every direction.

5

Thirty years after that, at night. She could feel it again now, the hairs on the back of her neck rising as she got closer to the edge.

"I should have come at night before. You were there, but I couldn't see you. It only works after the sun goes down. That's why I always saw you when I was dreaming.

"I wonder if I only noticed you because of the way I am, or if you made me that way. Like getting cancer from a cell phone, all that bad stuff hanging in the air, messing with my head.

"I'm sorry, I don't mean to be…" She stopped and laughed. "Yeah, like you care whether I'm sorry or not…

"It worked out all right anyway. I hate doctors, that's why I didn't want to get an abortion, I had a lot of trust issues related to that, but when it came down to it they just put me asleep. I woke up and everything was fine, they put her up for adoption.

"I was good after that, they put me on some medication and they thought that was it but it really wasn't. I just kind of decided I was going to act different. I stopped stealing, stopped lying, just did what people told me. Until now, anyway. I think I'm going to die pretty soon and I wanted to see you again. I've been in so many homes and hospitals and things, it's easy to get out once they trust you.

"They have these trains now, it's amazing how fast they are…

"You could show yourself if you wanted. The way you really are. I'd kind of like to see it. Go out with a bang."

Nothing happened and she laughed again.

"Or just listen. That'll be fine too."

She talked for a long time about what the hospital was like, the people she'd met, doctors and nurses and orderlies and other patients.

And then, not saying it yet but about to, still thinking, putting the words together:

I don't know why I'm telling you this. I know you don't care. You told me, it's the only thing you ever did tell me.

She imagined herself sleeping in a strange place, opening her eyes and seeing a spider crawling across her body. Her first reflex was to flatten it with her hand, but she hesitated. Maybe she wouldn't kill it. Maybe if she was in the right mood she'd just watch and see what it did, wonder what it was thinking.

The image in her mind got clearer. She felt sorry for the poor thing, trapped inside her brain with no place to go. Alone, like she was.

I'm the spider, Caroline realized.

She didn't want to die. She didn't want it to die… The whole thing was very confusing. She snapped out of it, returned to the real world, and there it was, standing on the ledge overlooking the lake.

"It will be simple."

What…

"The most beautiful thing I can think of."

And she started changing.

6

In a few days the infestation had completely swallowed northern Michigan. It was red and soft, like a fungus. Anything that tried to stop it was devoured.

Time passed. Tiny particles rose up into the air, mixing with the atmosphere and filtering the light of the sun into orange and violet. Vast canyons appeared, starting in the places where the land once met the ocean, twisting and turning from one hemisphere to the other.

The visitor continued to wait.

Veronica

It was two o'clock in the morning. Veronica knew for sure now that she was being followed. She'd circled the block three times, a quiet row of identical houses. There were no streetlights, no anything for at least half a mile in every direction except for the two of them, passing the same signs for the same real estate agency over and over again.

She switched off her headlights and turned to the right. She turned again, and kept turning, twisting back and forth, leaning gently on the gas pedal.

She rolled down her window as she tapped on the brake and took a deep breath. She couldn't do this when the car was moving, it made her dizzy, but now that she'd stopped it was like taking off a blindfold. Every tree was like a human face, a unique
signature fighting to be read through the pesticide and the fertilizers. She knew how many people lived in each house, where the dogs were walked. A half-empty beer can cut insistently through the night.

They were driving, that was new. She wondered if it had taken them as long as it had taken her, if it had scared them, who'd had to pin whose neck to the floor before somebody got behind the wheel.

She remembered her first time, stomping on the gas petal and letting the tires squeal as she circled around the parking lot...

They were still behind her. The beer can got closer, the smell got more and more obnoxious. She pulled over very suddenly and got out of the car. The beer can was on the ground under a soccer goal. She walked out into the middle of the field.

They parked their car behind hers, struggled to get it into park, and opened the doors hesitantly, like they were afraid it might not let them go. Their postures changed as their feet touched the grass, the spring came back to their step. There were four of them, all male, all bigger then she was. They fell into formation as they walked towards her, the tallest one in front and the other three behind him.

She didn't move, didn't look them in the eye, didn't do anything. The field was dark, but she could smell sweaty children, rotten apples under the trees. The leader stopped about twenty feet away. Two of the others circled around on either side of her.

The third dropped down onto his haunches. This wasn't an ordinary pack, it couldn't be, they'd already sent so many. All four of them were probably leaders themselves, probably pinned whelps' necks to the floor and fucked whoever it was they
wanted to fuck. But they were a pack now, for the moment. Somebody had to be the bitch. The leader smacked the bitch in back of the head and he scrambled out into the center of the circle they'd made. He spit on the dirt and clawed at it. He rose up for just a second to rub his soiled palms against his face and hiss, then turned around and stuck his butt in the air. He did it slowly, a little sexier than he would for just anyone. More feminine. He was making fun of her.

She didn't move, didn't react. She could smell their discomfort, the sweat on the back of their necks. This was not a small thing. You might have a display like this directed at you once or twice in your life, when you tried to push too far past your station or got too slow or lazy for the position you had. It was a humiliation. She should be foaming at the mouth, ready for violence.

But she was just standing there.

She was everything they'd heard - a monster, twisted inside beyond recognition. They were scared now, something new for them, maybe, maybe. She felt sorry for them.

The bitch scampered back behind the leader and they hesitated for a moment before they closed in. Veronica liked fighting, and she was better at it than anyone she knew, but sometimes it was just so easy. People would give you presents- their throat, or their rib, or their elbow, or the side of their head. All you had to do was take them. The one on the right ran towards her. His mouth was open; his tongue was hanging out and his fangs had emerged from their hiding places behind his teeth. He reached for her and she twisted her body, letting his arms go past her on either side. She stuck out her hand and dragged her nails down across his face. She smelled the blood, felt her own heart rate
spike and her fangs push against her gums. He cried out. She laughed and jabbed at his eyes with her fingertips.

She stepped to the side and pushed him backwards. He was screaming now. She heard feet shuffle on the dirt behind her, moving forward, hesitating as she drew blood, finding his courage and charging again just as she pulled his screaming packmate back towards her. They collided and fell over on top of one another. She cackled and kicked them both in the head until they stopped moving.

The leader was still standing there. He didn't know what to do. She saw the bitch's posture change. Why should he act like this when the leader didn't do his part? The bitch hissed. The leader didn't answer - another sign of weakness - and stepped forward, towards Veronica.

It was all she could do to keep her tongue from flopping from her mouth like a dog. Her fangs were bared and little bone spikes had emerged from her fingertips, splitting her skin and letting her blood mix with the others'. This was the best part, when all the juices were flowing. She tried to step outside of herself enough to enjoy it.

The leader tried to close the distance but he was slow, scared. The bitch hissed at him again. The leader turned away from Veronica and the two packmates stared into each other's eyes.

They pounced on one another simultaneously and started fighting. They rolled around in the dirt, trying to get their teeth onto one another's throats.

It took a second for Veronica to figure out how to respond. She picked a direction and ran like a deer through the soccer fields. Her claws and teeth retracted as her heart rate settled, and soon she was just a girl jogging.

She made her way to the edge of the neighborhood and crossed a street with four lanes, busy during the day but empty now, and stopped at the patch of grass dividing the road. She took a deep breath. She couldn't smell them, they hadn't followed her.

She lay down on the grass and started laughing. She couldn't help it. It was the most ridiculous thing she'd ever seen.

She recovered a few minutes later and got up. She only had a couple of hours left and had things to do, more things now that she'd gotten blood on her clothes. There was a Goodwill trailer in the corner of the parking lot of a nearby grocery store. The trailer was locked but there were cardboard boxes sitting outside of it. She dug through them, found a flannel shirt that fit her, and took a quick look around before she changed. She didn't care who saw her but she'd found that people looked at her funny when she didn't have all her clothes on.

There was a convenience store about a quarter mile away on the same road. It never closed. She walked there. She was tired already from the fight. She needed to get another car somehow, but that'd wait for tomorrow night.

She entered the store. The lights on the ceiling seemed impossibly bright. The cashier waved at her.

"Hello."

She smiled, nodded, and tried to get her tongue in the right position. This was embarrassing - even after all this time, the simple things were still hard. She finally squeezed it out.

"Hello."

She sounded like she had a cold. The cashier smiled back.

"The usual for you tonight, young lady?"

She nodded.

"Okay, okay, go ahead."

She smiled and went straight for the candy aisle. Her preference was for bright colors, anything sweet or sour or fruit-flavored. She avoided chocolate - she'd tasted it once when she'd bought a donut for the sprinkles and thought it was disgusting. She kept loading up until she couldn't carry anything else, dumped everything onto the counter, and turned towards the magazine rack. She returned holding a stack of magazines. The cashier rang her up. She dug into her pockets and pulled out a wad of bills. The cashier straightened them out one at a time and put her change down next to what she'd bought.

She took the bills and shoved them back into her pockets, but left the coins where they were.

"You know, it adds up when you leave those behind. If you don't want to take them that's fine, but they belong to you."

She smiled.

"Good-bye," she choked out, and left the store. The cashier watched her go.

It wasn't far from the store to where she slept. She'd made herself a small lair in the attic of a parking garage stairwell. It hadn't been disturbed yet, but if it ever was she'd just find another place. There was a pile of rags in the corner. She lay down on top of them and started eating.

She started out slow, holding each piece of candy up to the light coming in from the high corner-window, licking it and savoring the flavor before chomping it to dust. She reached into the other bag and pulled out her magazines, started flipping through them. She went through the tabloids quickly. Photography didn't interest her very much.

The comic books she saved for last. Her fingers seemed to vibrate as she opened the first one. She spent a lot of time on each page; she couldn't read, and was only dimly aware that she might be missing anything. She looked at the pictures, up close and from far away, right-side-up and upside down, watching them transform from things she hadn't seen before to things she had.

Her favorites had a girl with long black hair, just like hers. When she first saw them she ran to the cashier and pointed at the covers, too excited to speak.

The cashier just laughed.

"You like her? That's Veronica. Yeah, she looks just like you."

Veronica read and ate candy until she fell asleep. She woke up again as the night fell, smiling and remembering. Dreaming. Veronica like to fight, Veronica liked to drive. But this, this, this was what Veronica loved.

Iowa Highway

1

The first thing they did when they took a trip like this was pick new names. This time they were Michael and Jennifer. The house was empty when they got there; it was beautiful, the summer home of very wealthy people. The interior was an open shell, rugs on a stone panel floor with a kitchen in back and an open-sided spiral staircase that led up to a balcony bedroom and another set of stairs in back that led to a kitchen. The house was surrounded by grass, which was surrounded by woods, which were surrounded by a wooden fence.

They took their clothes off as soon as they got inside. Jennifer threw hers in the corner; Michael left a trail, starting with his shirt at the front door and ending with his underwear at the kitchen.

"Jesus, I'm hungry…" He stopped suddenly and looked at her sheepishly, like a dog that knows it's done something wrong. "No, I didn't mean…"

Jennifer shook her head. "I know you didn't. Don't worry."

She hoisted herself up onto the counter, put her hand on his shoulder, and tilted her head to the side.

He spit on her neck. His saliva was bright green; it hissed like oil in a frying pan, and a second later there was a swollen red mark on her neck. He nibbled on it gently, and her skin tore and split like tissue paper. She closed her eyes as he pressed his mouth against the wound.

They stayed at the house for about two weeks.

2

Jim had just passed the exit that would have led him home when the rain finally and definitively froze into hail. The sound of the ice hitting the roof of his truck got louder and harder, as though each individual stone were pissed off at him personally. He could barely see the road. Every story he had ever heard about somebody getting killed in a wreck started with weather like this.

He cursed and regretted it immediately. Taking the lord's name in vain. If he still owned his own truck there's no way in hell he'd still be driving tonight. He'd started with this crew because it'd be safer, he wouldn't have to worry about getting shafted every time fuel prices went up. At least when he was dead he wouldn't have to buy gas anymore.

He caught himself looking down at the speedometer as the exit got further behind him. If he didn't think of something else to think about he was going to go crazy.

Well. There was Joe and there was Petey. Really that was it, as far as people he had any regular contact with lately. His last conversation with Petey had gone so badly he automatically found himself leaning towards Joe, even though he hadn't even seen him in a couple of weeks. The three things that Joe talked about almost exclusively were politics, gambling, and sex, and he would usually touch on all three over the course of a conversation. Even bitching about their dispatcher wasn't enough to get him away from the holy trinity for more than a few minutes. Jim tried to remember where he'd started the last time they'd spoken.

"She's going to be on my dick like a dog on a pork chop."

Yeah, there it was. They were sitting in an odd corner of a truck stop south of the Quad Cities. They all ended up there a lot, they all worked for the same company and went to a lot of the same places. You sit for six hours, you see another guy wearing the same uniform you are, you start talking. The stools they were using were meant to go with a video game, a horse-racing simulator Jim never made any effort to understand and that he'd never seen anyone actually playing. It had become their regular spot to stop and talk whenever they ran into each other.

"You mean she's going to rip it off with her teeth?" Jim said.

Joe laughed a little longer than was strictly normal and kicked the steel pipe holding up the table. Jim couldn't remember who Joe'd been talking about that particular night, probably some waitress.

"Still, though, the time's coming. It's gonna fucking happen. It just is. Fucking destiny, my good friend."

"I'm sure it is, Joe."

"You don't believe me?"

"I believe everything you say, Joe. Always do."

Jim shifted in his seat as a giant mass passed through his peripheral vision, an obese man wearing a blue baseball cap walking slowly from the convenience store on one side of the compound to a collection of restaurants on the other. Joe waved.

"Hey, Pete."

The giant turned his head slightly in their direction, lifted his hand to acknowledge them, and kept walking. Joe didn't say anything until the big man entered the restaurant and left their sight. It was probably the longest Jim had ever heard him shut up.

"Now there's a fucked-up guy."

3

When they were done, Michael wiped off the counter with a washcloth and they went upstairs to find some new clothes. Jennifer found something she liked right away, a blue sun-dress. It took Michael longer. He settled on a pair of khaki pants and a green turtleneck. He also found a pair of glasses with round lenses. They made his vision blurry, so he broke the lenses and just wore the frames.

"I wonder who he is. He doesn't seem to own any suits, maybe he's a teacher." He could still cast a reflection in the bathroom mirror when all the lights were on and he stood in just the right place. He turned to the side and admired his profile. "That'd be a fun job, don't you think?"

Jennifer was looking at the pictures on the dresser, picking them up and putting them back down one at a time.

"Maybe he just doesn't like to wear suits when he's on vacation."

He left the bathroom. "You're probably right." He saw her lingering on one of the pictures, a seven-year-old girl playing soccer with a cousin or a younger brother. She was entranced, smiling with sad eyes. She noticed him watching and blushed.

"I'm sorry… I'm sorry…"

He looked away from her. "It's all right. Please don't worry."

He left the bedroom and went back downstairs. She followed a minute later. It was three o'clock in the morning.

"Do you want to go ahead and start now?"

Michael shook his head. "It's too late. It'd be suspicious. We should wait for tomorrow night. We can take a look at the property now, the sun won't rise for another couple of hours."

Jennifer looked out the window above the sink. "They say there's going to be a blizzard tomorrow night."

"They're wrong," Michael said. "I can hear it. It's not going to snow until later."

Michael was right. There wasn't a cloud in the sky the following evening.

4

Jim remembered. Joe'd been talking.

"I mean, he's a decent guy, but he was kind of messed up in the head before and he's really fucked now. He was in an accident and some people got killed, a whole family. Probably not his fault, but some fucking lawyer spewed a whole lot of shit and Petey doesn't know any better than to believe him, some guy, sounds smart…"

He saw Petey again about a day later at the same truck stop. It was freezing cold outside, and Petey was walking back and forth between the restrooms and the main entrance. Jim watched him haul his feet across the floor, one at a time, over and over again. Every so often he'd stop and sit down on the bench, and after a moment he would somehow find the strength to get back up and retrace his route a few more times.

A red streak darted across Jim's right rear-view mirror. A red sports car went flying past. Jim flinched. The car moved back into the left lane and slid more then halfway onto the shoulder before it got back on the road.

Jim felt his heartbeat smack the inside of his skull like a bass drum. That's it, he decided. I'm finishing the run and getting home in one piece. No more thinking about anything. Not Joe the asshole, not Petey the headcase, nobody.

He imagined saying the words 'Petey the headcase' to his wife and was ashamed of himself. He turned up the radio and looked for a new station.

5

They climbed up the side of the house together. From the roof they could see the rows flowing along the highway like water. Michael watched the cars, then turned and watched Jennifer. She was so beautiful. This was one of his favorite things, to be up here with her like this.

"How many more before we can get out of here?" she said.

Michael's heart fell through his chest. "I was thinking three," he said.

Jennifer didn't quite sigh. "All right. I think I can do that."

Michael looked back at the highway. "All right."

They stayed there, perched on the roof, for about two hours, until the traffic thinned out. They saw a truck roll by. There was nothing behind it or in front of it for more than two miles.

They glanced at each other, looked back down, and leapt into the air.

6

Jim was thinking about Petey again within an hour.

They saw each other again a few days after Joe had pointed Petey out. They were both standing by the window, watching the wind push the leaves back and forth across the parking lot. Neither was sure how long the other had been there. When they finally did notice each other, there was a moment of awkward silence.

"Hi, I'm Jim," Jim finally said. Petey didn't say anything for a long moment. Jim wondered if he was making a fool of himself.

"I'm Petey," he finally responded.

"Well, all right," Jim said, still not sure where he stood. "Nice to meet you. You know Joe, right?"

Petey paused again before he spoke, and Jim realized that it wasn't anything personal, this was just how he talked.

"Yeah."

He looked out the window again.

"Joe's an asshole."

It took a second for it to sink in, and then Jim laughed out loud, a deep belly laugh that embarrassed him as soon as he got it under control.

"Well, I guess that's about right. Sure does like to talk, though."

"Yeah," Petey said.

They only talked for a little while longer before they had to get going, but the next time they saw each other they had more time to spare.

7

Michael saw the truck on the side of the road and a man in flannel standing next to it, kicking the right front tire and swearing up a blue streak. In the darkness, he could see the truck driver long before the driver could see him, and even when he was in sight it took the driver a long time to notice him.

"Do you have a problem?" Michael said.

He stopped kicking the tire.

"I do. My truck just died and won't start up again, my radio is dead, and my cell phone isn't working."

He looked up at Michael, suddenly suspicious.

"Mind if I ask what you're doing out here at midnight?"

Michael licked his lips and looked him in the eye.

"Relax."

The driver's posture changed instantly. His shoulders dropped and his hands fell limp at his sides.

"It doesn't look like you're going to be able to get back on the road tonight. My home isn't far from here. You can spend the night there and call a mechanic in the morning."

The driver looked at his truck, then back at Michael.

"Sounds good."

Michael turned around and started walking back towards the house.

"What's your name again?"

"Joe," the driver said.

About half an hour later they approached the front gate and followed the driveway to the house. The porch lights came on as they got closer, revealing a heavy oak front door, painted a dark wine red. Jennifer opened the door from inside the house.

"We have a guest."

She looked Joe over.

"Do you want something to eat?" she asked.

Joe nodded his head and stumbled into the house. The table had been set with the dark gray stoneware dishes they'd found in the kitchen cabinets. There was a giant wooden serving bowl filled with pasta and broiled tomatoes and a small plate with a neat pile of grated parmesan cheese on top of it. Joe sat down and started eating. Every few minutes Jennifer would ask him a question about his job or what his interests were, but he was never able to give a coherent answer. Eventually Michael told him he was done eating and that he should go downstairs.

It was a tiny bedroom, just large enough to contain a king-sized bed and a nightstand. Jim went inside, closed the door behind him, collapsed onto the bed, and wondered where he was and what he was doing. Then he fell asleep.

He woke up a while later with a clear head. Not much time had passed; it was still dark outside.

He blinked and jumped back. Jennifer was perched on the corner of the bed. He'd somehow failed to notice that she was there.

"Hello," she said. Joe was very confused.

"It was nice talking to you at dinner." She paused on the odd chance that he might have something to say and started up again when he just kept staring. "We don't get much company, and it's not often I get to talk to someone other than my husband.

"There was something else I didn't have a chance to mention, something I was hoping you could help me with."

Again, she hesitated, and again, nothing.

"I want a child."

Joe's jaw dropped, very slightly.

He woke up again a few hours later, not much better rested. The sun was starting to rise outside, and orange light shone on the door of the bedroom through the window. For a second he was certain that he'd been having a dream, but he could feel Jennifer's naked body pressing against his, her hands resting on his stomach. He wondered how he was going to tell this story and not sound like a complete liar. It was easier when you just made stuff up.

He closed his eyes and appreciated the novelty of her body heat. He moved his arm, and felt something warm and wet on the side of his body. He freed his hand from the covers and held it up to the light creeping through the window. It was covered with blood.   He climbed out of bed and saw a long red smear starting with a tear in his skin just below his ribs and continuing down to his knees.

The door opened and Michael stepped into the room. He was completely naked except for his glasses, and there was not yet enough light to hide the fact that his green eyes were glowing gently in the dark.

"You must be pleased with yourself," he whispered, sneering. He said it again, shifting the emphasis to the last three syllables.

8

Jim and Petey ended up talking pretty regularly. They could not be described as good friends, and Jim had no desire to ever meet Petey outside of a bar or a truck stop. But they became familiar with each other.

Jim never talked to Petey about his faith, both because the subject never came up and because Jim was not comfortable talking to people about God outside of church. It wasn't a problem Leanne had, and he was grateful for that. If he hadn't been lucky enough to be one of the hundreds of people she'd gotten in the face of over the years, he knew he never would've met her.

He remembered: They were walking through woods near their house on a Sunday afternoon, talking about how they'd met, what their lives had been like before and how things were going to be different now that they were married. Jim had been able to take two weeks off of work right after the wedding, but he'd had to stay on the road for a month afterward, and he had harbored a fear that once she saw how often he wouldn't be around, she'd have second thoughts about being with him. But it hadn't taken long to realize it wasn't going to be a problem for her. Leanne missed him when he was away, but she still had friends and church and long walks and nieces and nephews in town to keep her busy. She was all right.

He was the problem. He'd had the job so long he could barely remember doing anything else and he'd learned how to let the miles go by. But now every minute he was on the road was a minute he couldn't spend with her, and it was driving him crazy.

He felt weak and stupid, telling her this. The leaves had turned brown and orange and red, matching Leanne's hair, and they'd held hands like teenagers.

"It sounds like you don't like your job that much." She said it with a sly smile on her face; she'd been insisting that he wasn't satisfied with what he was doing for as long as they'd known each other, and he'd always denied it up and down.

Jim smiled back, not quite blushing. "There's nothing wrong with it, it just doesn't feel like I'm doing much anymore."

"Maybe you should find more things to do. Maybe there's somebody you can help out."

He denied the possibility repeatedly for five minutes. Then, finally, and only to exclude him from consideration, he mentioned Petey.

"Well there you go," Leanne said.

He saw Petey two weeks later, looking out the same window where they'd first spoke. It was late in the afternoon, and clouds darkened the sky even though the sun hadn't set yet. Jim's truck - the company's truck, he reminded himself - was at the warehouse. It was supposed to have been unloaded two hours ago. If that actually happened before today became tomorrow it would be a blessing.

Jim said hello, and Petey nodded his head in acknowledgement. They talked about the weather for a little while.

"Look," Jim finally said. "I was hoping I could talk to you about something. Do you go to church?"

There was a long pause. Jim was used to that, but this one went on even longer then usual, and toward than end of it he found himself growing uncomfortable.

"Why do you ask?" Petey said, with more thought behind his words than usual.

Jim felt a sharp twist in the pit of his stomach but pushed past it.

"I heard about your accident. Something like that can mess a man up."

Jim glanced away from the window and saw that Petey was staring right at him.

"I don't believe in that shit," Petey said. He turned around and walked away. It wasn't until he was gone that Jim realized the conversation was over.

9

Petey was driving. It was a beautiful, clear night; it was late and the road was empty. He'd been six hours late getting cut loose from the warehouse. He realized that anybody else would be pissed if they had to drive through the night like this but it didn't make any difference to him. He wasn't listening to the radio; he hadn't done that in months, at first because he was afraid of getting distracted and later because the sound of people's voices started bothering him.

Two and a half hours went by.

The engine died. The lights on the dashboard went out a second later, and for a few seconds he felt like a blind man.

He opened the door to the cab, took a look at his rear-view mirror to make sure there weren't any other cars coming, and climbed down. He turned around and saw a man with green eyes standing on the side of the road. Somehow he'd failed to see him in the mirror.

"I see you're having some engine trouble."

10

There was a knock on the door. Jennifer put her clothes back on and answered it. Michael was there; he'd brought someone with him, a very large man in a winter coat.   The first thing she did was look at his face. Different people responded to her husband's control in different ways. Some of them sleepwalked silently, others would act drunk and say things they usually wouldn't.

"His name's Petey," Michael said, and pushed him through the door. "Go to the table and eat what we put in front of you."

Dinner was already served, a plate of cold pasta drowned in sauce. Petey started eating.

"Do you like your job, Petey?" Jennifer asked him.

"No," he said, in an even voice.

"Then why do you do it?"

He didn't answer.

"Because he can't do anything else, that's why they all do whatever they're doing." Michael was sitting at the table, hunched over, staring idly at the countertop.

"No. I don't have to."

Petey answered quickly, leaving no space in between Michael's words and his response, but without changing his tone of voice. He put the silverware down on the table and stared off into space.

"I'd have to get a gun. That's the only sure way. Even with pills, you can make a mistake and it doesn't work right. I could get a gun at a pawnshop, I don't think they cost that much…"

He shook his head back and forth, looked down at his plate, and continued eating as though nothing had happened.

11

When he was done eating, Michael led him away from the table and brought him to the basement bedroom.

"Stay here," he said. "Sleep." He closed the door.

Petey collapsed onto the bed. He was confused and very tired. He wanted to sleep, but he was scared to close his eyes. Something he'd said at the dinner table, he couldn't even remember what it was now.

He needed to walk, Petey decided. He hadn't gotten any exercise all day. He could hear Mike and Jennifer arguing on the balcony as he came upstairs. Neither of them seemed to notice as he left the house.

He saw something as he stepped off the driveway onto the grass, a pair of lines cutting across the field, barely visible in the darkness, like an old scar. He approached them, leaned over and touched the dirt with his fingers. Somebody had driven a car across the field.

The trail led towards the woods. As it approached the trees it split into several shallower tracks, cutting the grass into a dirty mess. There were vehicles wedged between the tree trunks wherever they would fit.

Petey heard a voice he recognized.

"Hello? Please god, you've got to help me…"

He found Joe naked and tied to a tree. His body was covered with blood and chemical burns, and there were corpses tied to the trees around him.

"What happened?" Petey whispered.

Joe laughed, emptying his lungs to do it, and told him everything. For a moment he forgot where he was. He closed his eyes, and when he opened them Petey was walking away.

"Wait..."

His head dropped and his eyes closed again.

12

And suddenly, just sitting there driving a truck he'd spent countless hours driving and remembering an afternoon he'd thought about many times already, Jim just fucking hated all of it, the truck and the snow falling around him and his fucking job and his fucking life.

There was a flash in the sky up ahead, heat lightning, and before his eyes could recover he saw a pair of black silhouettes flying through the air towards his truck, a man and a woman. The sky went dark again and the silhouettes were gone.

His engine went dead, and his dashboard lights faded out a few minutes later. He pulled the truck to the side of the road. The radio didn't work and neither did his cell phone. He wondered if he was going to get fired.

He didn't allow himself to admit what he'd seen until a few minutes had passed. He leaned against his trailer and watched the snow fall, while he thought about it. Suddenly, a smile appeared on his face, and the tension disappeared from his shoulders. He figured it out. He laughed at himself, at how long it had taken him.

A man with green eyes appeared on the other side of the road. Jim wasn't sure where he'd come from. Just looking at the man made Jim dizzy.

"I see you're having some engine trouble," the man said.

"Yeah," Jim answered, because it was the truth and because he didn't see any reason not to.

"It doesn't look like you're going to be able to get back on the road tonight. My home isn't far from here. You can spend the night and call a mechanic in the morning."

Jim thought about it for a second and shook his head no.

"I'm sorry, but I can't. I'm just going to leave the truck here and walk to the nearest gas station so I can call my wife and have her pick me up."

The man with the green eyes seemed confused.

"It's a long way to walk in the cold. Wouldn't you rather come with me?"

Jim thought about it.

"No," he finally responded. "It's nice of you to offer, but I can't. God sent two angels to fuck with my engine." He wouldn't usually have sworn, but he was feeling strangely uninhibited tonight. "He wants me to quit my job so I can spend more time with my wife. I was worried before about finding another job, but I'm pretty sure things will work out okay. And I'm not worried about the cold. Thanks anyway."

He turned away from the green-eyed man, took a step back in the direction of the last gas station he'd seen, and started walking.

He thought about what he had said. It was a little embarrassing, but he meant every word. He'd seen angels. They were different than any pictures of angels he'd seen, but that didn't really surprise him.

His truck disappeared behind him as the lights of the gas station became visible through the snow.

13

Jennifer came downstairs a few minutes later. She saw Petey's boots up against the wall outside the bedroom. They were covered with mud and pine needles.

She opened the door. Petey was pretending to sleep. She stepped inside and closed the door behind her.

"Open your eyes," she said, and Petey did.

"You were outside."

Petey didn't admit it or deny it, he barely moved.

"Why did you come back? You know what's going to happen, right?"

It took a while for Petey to put the words together.

"It doesn't sound so bad."

He looked up at the ceiling.

"It's not like I have much to look forward to, anyway."

For a moment he felt as though he had suddenly become transparent, that she was watching something underneath him that he wasn't able to see himself.

She pulled her dress up over her head and dropped it on the floor by the foot of the bed. She wasn't wearing anything underneath; her body was lean and willowy, and seemed to hang from her shoulders like a curtain.

She climbed onto the bed, let her weight settle on top of him, and kissed him on the lips.

14

About an hour later, Michael came downstairs. When he opened the door Petey was asleep in bed and Jennifer was sitting in a corner of the room with her arms wrapped around her knees.

She looked up at him without fear.

"Not this time," she said quietly. "Just don't."

He was confused. He was actually angrier than before, but his face was quiet and his body was still.

"Fine," he eventually said.

He reached for his neck with both hands.

"I'll make it quick."

The Invasion

The direction of Donnie's life had taken a lot from him, but one of the things it had given him back was time. Time to think, time to reconstruct what had gone wrong. Leaning against the fence near his apartment with the friends circumstances had forced him to make, staring into space, he found himself circling back around to three particular conversations. They were the conversations that had put him where he was now. They were the big ones.

First - it was Thanksgiving, his older brother's house. Donnie was in the kitchen. He pulled a Mountain Dew out of a Styrofoam cooler and heard his little nephew Jimmy laughing behind him. He turned around, smiling. The picture of himself that Donnie carried in his mind was of a good uncle, someone with a bit more authority and distance than an older brother but also a dispenser of noogies and piggy-back rides. He was a young buck, still untamed, but with the basic qualities that would later flower into fatherhood. A young man, but a man.

"What are you laughing at?" Donnie said. Little Jimmy pointed at the can his uncle was holding and laughed some more.

"You know what that does, right Uncle Donnie?"

"No, kid, why don't you tell me?"

"You know."

"No, I don't." Then he remembered. "Oh, you're worried you're not gonna get any cousins if I drink too much?" Little Jimmy kept laughing. Donnie put the can down on the counter and got Jimmy in a headlock; they wrestled for the short time it took Donnie to pin Jimmy to the ground and tickle him.

"Well if it makes you feel better, I'll try something else." Donnie got up and pulled out another can at random. The can was bright purple, almost pink. It was called Bermuda Juice, and it was not a brand of soda Donnie had ever seen before. He opened it and took a sip.

It was delicious. As soon as he finished one, he wanted another. He drank more then a dozen over the course of the holiday, a number matched by most of the other men in the family. Bermuda Juice was really good soda. Over the course of the next few months, Bermuda Juice would become Donnie's favorite beverage, supplanting any other kind of soft drink and even beer. His reaction was not unusual. Everybody loved Bermuda Juice.

Second - three years later. Donnie had married Sandy. It didn't bother him that they were both young. Donnie had had sex with many women, and his sexual potency was widely acknowledged, by his brother and his friends, and more subtly by his parents and co-workers. If he wanted to settle down at an early age, no one would ever think it was because he was surrendering or because he could no longer compete in the marketplace. That part of his life had simply run its course. It was time for him to move on.

He'd wanted to get started on a family as soon as possible, and it was here that his plans hit a snag. Donnie couldn't get Sandy pregnant. They'd seen doctors and had tests performed, but nothing seemed to be physically wrong with either of them. It just wasn't happening.

It was late at night. Donnie had left their bedroom to go and get a consolatory post-coital can of Bermuda Juice. When he got back Sandy was watching the Tonight Show. The much-anticipated Masterlord Xenomorph/Alicia Silverstone interview was on tonight, and it was an open secret that they were planning on publicly announcing their sexual relationship.

The aliens had made their presence known months ago. The impact of the big reveal had been largely blunted by the rumors that had been steadily gaining in volume for almost a year prior to that; by the time of their press release, everybody knew the score already and to dwell on the matter any further was considered unsophisticated. The aliens had taken refuge on our planet a few years ago, had disguised themselves as human beings and large dogs until they could be sure of their safety, and had covertly started several businesses in order to earn a living in their new home. They were peaceful, and, after revealing themselves, completely open and candid about all their activities. No one had any real problem with them.

This didn't mean people were entirely comfortable with the idea of human/alien sex. Again, there had been rumors, whispers on the margins of society, but people didn't really know, didn't have to confront their feelings on the subject if they didn't want to.

Donnie and Sandy watched the interview and turned off the set shortly afterward.

"Fucking weird," Donnie said.

"I don't know," Sandy responded. "They aren't hurting anyone."

"Fucking weird," Donnie repeated. "I wonder what she's getting out of it."

"Well, she's back in the news. It'll probably be good for her career. But I don't think it's that, really, I think there are some real feelings there. You saw them, they're in love."

"I can't believe I'm listening to this."

"It's not so strange. Masterlord is the leader of his species, he's powerful, women are attracted to that. And there's just something about him. He's got presence, you know?"

"Well, I'm sorry if I'm not…"

He stopped. He realized that he'd raised his voice, and that Sandy was giving him the look she gave him when he was banished to the couch. He didn't bother arguing, he knew the routine, it had been happening often enough lately. He left the room.

There was a part of him that was glad he no longer shared a bed with his wife all that often anymore. It made it easier to hide that it was getting harder for him to get an erection.

Third - months later. Alicia Silverstone was guaranteed box-office gold. Her relationship with the Masterlord had come to an end, but her association with the Xenomorphs had carried over into a successful series of romantic comedies revolving around human/alien couplings. It was not quite a hundred percent acceptable for a human woman to openly express desire for an alien, but you could drop hints, you could make jokes about what 'they' 'could do' or 'were capable of'. It was a running joke on The View.

The media was behind the curve. Donnie had long suspected this to be true, and conversation at a recent fraternity reunion he'd attended had confirmed it. At least three of his brothers had admitted to him that they suspected their wives or girlfriends were fucking Xenomorphs on the sly, and he was sure there were many more who were either clueless about what was going on or were scared to admit it. The threat was real. And in Donnie's case, it was greatly magnified by his failure to perform, a secret shame he was certain was unique to him and which he had not shared with anyone.

Romantic love had never played a large part in Donnie's worldview, not even when his relationship with Sandy had gotten serious; as far as he'd been concerned the two of them were doing what came naturally, and no further explanation was needed. But now he embraced the idea with the fanaticism of the recently converted. Sandy would not cheat on him because he and Sandy were in love. In all of existence, there was only Sandy for Donnie, and only Donnie for Sandy. Their special connection would overcome all obstacles.

This bond between them, if it ever existed at all, was destroyed by Donnie's discovery of a thin layer of translucent green slime covering the back seat of the convertible he'd bought her as an anniversary present. He confronted her when she got home from work, expecting either tears or angry denials. Instead, she seemed relieved.

"I'm a woman, Donnie," she said, her tone suggesting he might not know what that meant. "I have needs."

She left to go stay with her mother. Not long after, Donnie was served with divorce papers. Sandy got the house.

Upon returning to the single life, Donnie found that he was not alone. The bars and bowling alleys and vacant lots of the city were full of guys like him, all with different versions of the same story. Together, they watched the world change around them. Human-on-human sex was increasingly regarded as an understandable but less then realistic fantasy, like participating in a racially diverse threesome. Even the pornography that occupied more and more of Donnie's time tended to feature aliens now. They were talking about giving them citizenship so that they could run for office. It was increasingly difficult to take human politicians seriously as their wives ran out on them one after the other.

Donnie stood up long enough to put his hands in his pockets, then leaned back against the fence. He listened to the chatter of the men around him. They were mostly talking about who was gay and who wasn't. Many of them had openly turned to homosexuality, but not as many as you might think. It was much more common to keep what you were doing a secret; the guys who were the most eager to throw accusations around were inevitably the ones who were up to something themselves. For Donnie, sneaking off with another guy was still a bridge too far, but he wasn't as certain about it now as he had been even a month ago. He was lonely.

With the speed and suddenness of a gunshot, all conversation ceased. Donnie jumped and looked around. It was almost too much to hope for; he prayed it wasn't a false alarm.

It wasn't. It was a woman, walking down the sidewalk. Her hips were wide and bulged out in an odd way, and her face was pock-marked and asymmetrical, each of her cheeks curving in a slightly different fashion. But none of that mattered. She was here, actually physically present. She was a woman. Woman woman woman woman. She was showered with whistles and hey-babies as she walked past, pausing every so often to give the gift of a half-smile before she kept going.

A black limousine pulled up about a block ahead of her, and an alien got out. The aliens looked more or less like what the Roswell posters and cable documentaries and many seasons of the X-Files had taught everyone to expect, the main difference being their height (they were all somewhere between six and seven feet tall) and the skeletal broadness of their shoulders, which made their bodies look T-shaped when they were undressed and like inverted triangles when they wore the tailored suits they increasingly favored.

The alien looked back and forth, his neck twitching as he changed the direction of his gaze. His face was completely expressionless. He opened one of the rear doors of the car as the woman approached. She smiled at him shyly and bent over to climb inside.

The Xenomorph smacked her on the ass. She giggled. She got into the car, the alien slammed the door shut and they drove off.

There was a moment of silence. It subsided, and the men of earth continued their sad conversation.

Mario and Luigi and the Lords of the Sky

Mario and his little brother Luigi had both gotten their names from listening to children, from pushing their ears against the screen back-doors of houses while the little humans gathered around their glowing screens. Harriet had gotten hers, she said, from a tombstone. Mario had no way to verify that, he couldn't read. Bad enough he had named himself and was attending meetings. The line had to be drawn somewhere.

The humans drove in cars and built roads for the cars to go on, made ice cream appear somehow and then kept it locked away where it was hardly ever accessible, built houses and put bright shiny things inside of them and then locked their doors. They had everything now, the whole world. It had to stop.

Harriet held her meetings under an oak tree inside a graveyard that had been hidden inside of a mall parking lot. It was a safe place; the humans were unwilling or unable to clear away the tombstones. It was out in the open but easy to miss; the humans wanted not to see it, wanted to park their cars and get to the mall and come back and go home without thinking any more then they had to.

Mario had been to Harriet's meetings before, but this was Luigi's first time.

"Hello," Harriet said to Luigi as they settled down on the bed of leaves under the tree. "I haven't met you before."

"Hello," Luigi answered.

Harriet got up and rubbed her body against the bark of the tree.

"We're moving forward. I've found a way."

She finished rubbing and leaped over the fence. The others followed her; only Luigi hesitated. They were a group, they were supposed to do things together, that was how it worked. It was a new concept for them, adopted out of necessity. Mario and Luigi had at least had each other, since they'd been young they'd stayed together. The others were loners.

If you were watching you'd see seven cats making their way across the parking lot together, but you'd only have a second to notice them before they made it to the grass and disappeared. They travelled like that, disappearing and briefly reappearing as they crossed a road or a patch of pavement, until they reached a very long and narrow stretch of woods bordering a bike path.

They weren't cats. They looked like cats, but they weren't. There wasn't a name for what they were.

They passed through a tunnel that led under a set of train tracks. On the inside of the tunnel was a message written in enthusiastic teenage letters with orange spray paint.

HE THAT MAKES A MONSTER OF HIMSELF TAKES AWAY THE PAIN OF BEING A MAN.

-HUNTER S. THOMPSON

They went through the tunnel without reading the message, went back into the woods, and made their way to a small yellow brick building that was connected to the bike path by a service road. The road was blocked by a barbed wire fence. They climbed the trees next to the fence and made long leaps down to the ground, landing in a popcorn rhythm. The door to the building was supposed to be locked with a padlock but it wasn't; Harriet opened it; the smell of rust from the door gave way to a combination of animal shit and chemicals, and then more rust as they went inside. There were pipes everywhere, gauges, cranks and levers.

There was a dead human woman with red hair lying face down in the back corner of the building. She was wearing a black dress that had been torn open in the process of killing her; there were long claw marks raking across her spine and blood everywhere. A play kill, not a hunter's kill, it had taken a while. Above her, taped to the wall with masking tape, were pictures of skyscrapers torn from magazines. There was a train schedule in her hand.

Harriet circled the body with prancing footsteps, showing off.

"She was a witch. She wanted a friend."

She laughed, they all did, it was funny.

The witch had spent a lot of time with Harriet before Harriet had killed her, and had explained many things about how human beings had taken hold of the world. They'd met in the pump house because the witch hadn't wanted her husband to find out that she was a witch. That was funny too but they didn't laugh, they were being serious now.

"The ones who the others follow live high above the clouds," Harriet said. "They stay in towers and look down on everyone else."

"The towers cannot be climbed like a tree. We'll have to climb them from the inside. We won't be able to hide. We'll need disguises." It was too much too soon, too many new ideas. Harriet went over it a few more times and tried to make it clear what she meant. The other listened attentively.

She climbed on top of the dead woman. She rolled around in her blood and said words that none of the others had heard before, words the witch had taught her.

She did that for a long time. Harriet slowly disappeared, faded like fog in a window after the sun comes up.

The woman with the red hair opened her eyes and stood. The scars on her back had healed. She did not move like a human being. She moved like Harriet.

Luigi gasped. Mario bit at his ear to shut him up before he embarrassed himself.

She showed them what to do. They took the bodies one at a time, as people rode by on their bikes, falling from the trees onto them and dragging their bodies back to the pump house. They had not changed, they could do everything they could do before. Only their skins were different.

They left the pump house and followed Harriet, walking in plain sight, terrifying all of them except her. They followed her because she was the leader; they were all still new to this, but they were fairly certain that when the leader walked, they should follow. They passed a library, stopped at a crosswalk. A girl with a braid in her hair pointed out that they were wearing their clothes inside out. They took their clothes off, fixed the problem, put their clothes back on and kept going. The girl ran away.

They waited for the train and got on board without incident. The minute that the doors closed and the box started moving, they all began to wonder if they had made a mistake. This was strange, being carried like this. There was no way to tell for sure where they were being taken.

"It's like being food that's been eaten that's still moving," one of them said, and the others nodded - they all knew what that was like.

"We're still a group," Harriet said. "We have a plan. An agreement."

They sat where they were uncomfortably. It was the middle of the day and they had the car to themselves.

"Look," Harriet said, and pointed out the window. The tower had appeared over the horizon. "That's where we're going. That's where we're going to kill them."

A fat man in a dark blue uniform came by and asked for their tickets. When they didn't answer, he told them they had to pay money or get off the train. He was still bored at this point; when they continued to ignore him he got upset and raised his voice. Mario grabbed his throat and squeezed as hard as he could, until the man stopped moving. They were hungry and wanted to eat him but the witch had told Harriet that that would attract attention, so they put his body in the bathroom instead.

They got off the train twenty minutes later. It took them more than an hour to leave the train station - the noise at the platform was disorienting, and made it harder to contend with the spinning doors that led to the train station, and once they got past that they still had to work up the nerve to ride the escalator. They went out onto the street, and for the first time they felt the cold. The buildings towered overhead, the people rushed by, ignoring them or briefly glancing at them in annoyance for breaking the flow of the crowd. There were no places to hide.

"We're a group," Harriet repeated urgently, and set out in the direction of the tower. The group followed her. Mario and Luigi kept to the rear this time, closer to each other than any of the others.

They passed a hamburger restaurant on their way to the tower. The smell that filled the air had no relationship to anything any of them would consider food. They kept going.

They made it.

"Who?" Mario asked, as they looked up.

"All of them," Harriet answered. "We need to make sure."

There was a line of people leading out from the building and going around the block. They started with the end of the line and moved forward. A large German man in a Hawaiian shirt was the first to die.

They only got a few of them, the rest ran away. They didn't mind; the ones they wanted were at the top. As long as they kept going up and didn't let anyone get past them, they'd be fine.

They were wandering around the lobby looking for the stairs when the police opened fire.

Panic, jumping and hiding and running. Screaming metal ripping through the air. Luigi never saw where it was that Mario died, if he was one of the three or four whose heads and chests exploded in the initial barrage or if they got him as they leapt and pounced back and forth down the street trying to get away.

Harriet and Luigi made it to the lakefront. They climbed a tree and hid there. Harriet said the words that made their second skins melt away, made them smaller, made them harder to find.

But not impossible. They had both seen it, the others' bodies changing as they died. The humans knew what they were looking for now. A secret that had always been, destroyed in a few artless minutes.

Harriet had been shot in the shoulder, and was bleeding. Luigi was untouched.

"Mario," Luigi whispered, and then there was a long silence between them, which Harriet tentatively broke.

"It was the group," she said. "We all decided. It was an idea. It was more important than Mario was."

Luigi did not wait more than a moment before he dove at her throat with his teeth.

He left her in the tree, strung over the branch. He left his name behind with her.

The next few years were hard ones, full of cats strung up on poles and hiding places burning to the ground. But they never caught him.

Dress Rehearsal

A significant sub-theme of Vincent George's autobiography was the frequency with which really and truly momentous shit would happen to him while he was walking his dog and talking on the phone. One hand on the leash and the other pressing the cell to the side of his head. He never got a headset, it was a superstition.

"Well, yeah it'll be expensive, things are expensive now, you might have noticed, the audience is very small these days... Yeah, my kids will go for it, it's new, it's shiny, they'll go for it..." Vincent George didn't have any children, he was a talent manager. "Well, how creepy could it be if Uncle Vinny thinks it's okay, I mean they don't know quantum physics from... yeah, yeah. This will happen, okay? It's a good idea you had, I'm glad you came to me before you decided to do something useful with it. You're a marvel, I mean that."

Vincent George walked his dog around the inside edge of the barrier. Green grass on his side, on the other side not so much grass.

Vincent George was comfortable walking the edge. It was another theme of his autobiography, he hoped a subtle one.

He saw a woman and a child on the other side. They were far gone, their skins were covered with blisters and their eyelids were swollen nearly shut. Vincent kept walking. They stayed where they were.

The following day Vincent had lunch five times, once by himself (Vincent was edgy, Vincent was deep), three times with guys like himself, and once with Claire. Claire was one of Vincent's kids.

"That's the thing exactly, kiddo, what this lets them do, it lets them get a little closer. They want to be closer, all the shit in the world, they want to be right there with you, but there's only one of you."

"But..."

He didn't let her finish. Claire, in her not-so-secret-heart of not-so-secret-hearts, really wanted to be a movie star. One of the first things she bought when she really started getting paid was a hat that Audrey Hepburn used to wear. She was a retro kid, it gave her something cute to talk about in interviews.

"...this is different than the movies. Movies are still a niche thing, sweety, you know I can't do that for you. People want skin, especially your skin, sweet cheeks, make no mistake." That got a smile. Skin was a big deal these days. "They want smells that don't smell like medical waste. They don't want a picture. They want you, they all want you all of the time. And now we can give you to them."

She looked cute and confused. "I still don't feel like I know what you're talking about."

"That's because I haven't told you yet. It's a development, something brand new. Quantum physics."

He told her, she didn't believe him. He'd expected that. They made another appointment for Thursday.

The lab was white and antiseptic, not Claire's kind of place. They put her in the booth.

"Just hold still for a second, kiddo... okay, great, now start the monologue."

She did her big scene. Claire's breakout character was Dr. Georgia Haskins, an intrepid investigator for the National Special Health Service.

"We don't keep the wall up because we want to. We do it because we have no choice. We are the last line of defense - you have the luxury of getting offended by the decisions I have to make, but..."

"That'll do, sweet cheeks," Vincent said. "Come on out of the booth, now."

They ate sandwiches while the lab boys did their thing, then they came back to the booth. Somebody pushed a button.

There was no noise, no smell, and only a short, soft, modest flash of blue light indicating that the machine had been activated.

The booth was empty, and then there was Claire.

"We don't keep the wall up because we want to. We do it because we have no choice. We are the last line of defense - you have the luxury of getting offended by the decisions I have to make, but..."

Not an image, not a hologram, her. It was something you could feel, just looking at her. This was a person. The second Claire got as far into the monologue as Claire originally had, then they turned the machine off.

Claire stood completely still on the other side of the room with her mouth hanging slightly open, staring at the empty booth. Vincent was smiling even more then usual.

"Cool, huh?"

She recovered enough to get some words out.

"I could have touched her..."

"You could have. But it would have been a bad idea. It's complicated. Quantum physics."

"What would have happened if you kept the machine turned on after I was done talking? Would she have still disappeared? Can... you said she's not a hologram, what's she thinking? Is she thinking? Can she see us?"

"These are some fascinating philosophical questions you're asking here, Claire. I was hoping we could grab an early dinner and go over all of this stuff."

They spent most of dinner talking about licensing. Vincent had the contracts ready. She signed, all was well.

They thought it would be too expensive, they thought it would freak people out. Vincent was right, they were wrong. Vincent was magnanimous about it in his book. They recorded the shows live in

Chicago every week and reproduced them via quantum synthesis in Boston, L.A., Madison, Nashville, Miami, and eventually New York after the riots stopped and they got the barrier set up there again. It took a while for the city to repopulate and they took a loss at first, but in the long term it was a good move. Nobody wanted to see Manhattan get completely overtaken by the bug.

There were other wrinkles - little things, not big things. Vincent only saw one of them personally. He was watching the preview of the new show in Nashville. They were right up in the fourth act. Vincent was the only one there who wasn't part of the crew, they wanted to make sure everything was working before they had a real audience to deal with. Dr. Georgia Haskins was stalking a gang of smugglers through an abandoned warehouse. The set was nice, big and set up so that it looked even bigger, getting the point of darkness across without actually obscuring the audience's view of what was happening. Vincent looked down into the pit and munched on popcorn as Georgia came closer and closer to stepping into the smugglers' trap.

The alarm started ringing. It wasn't part of the show. They wouldn't kid about that. Dr. Georgia Haskins and the three smugglers continued their dance.

Vincent had a bag of popcorn balanced precariously on the railing that divided the theater seating from the pit. This was another one of his edgy habits, it wasn't something the tech people would let just anybody get away with. When the alarm rang out, he jumped out of his seat quickly and started looking for the exit. In the process he spilled his popcorn down onto the stage.

He froze, and watched the kernels of popcorn fall down onto the set. One of them landed on Dr. Georgia Haskins' shoulder.

She looked up at him.

That was enough to break the script - when she stopped doing what she was supposed to do the smugglers started looking around too. They heard the sirens and quickly ran away, escaping through the doors by which they had entered the stage.

"What's going on?" She was still in character.

"Claire?" Vincent didn't know how this worked, he wasn't a fucking scientist.

"That's not my name," said Dr. Georgia Haskins.

"Look, I understand your dedication, sweetheart, but we're in the middle of an emergency, nobody's watching..."

Dr. Georgia Haskins stared at him silently, completely in control and very pissed off.

Vincent cleared his throat. "The barrier came down. We've got to get out of here."

She thought about it for a moment. She jumped up and hoisted herself over the railing.

"Go. I'll follow." The bright red emergency signs were all lit up, letting them know where they had to go to make it to the evacuation. Vincent ran, he heard her footsteps behind him.

They were almost there. They came to a main intersection of two hallways. The signs told Vincent to turn left and he did.

He heard Dr. Georgia Haskins' voice behind him.

"Stop right where you are."

He turned around. She had her gun drawn. She held it with purpose, as though it did not contain blanks. She was facing a group of four invaders. They were all bad cases, only one of them still had a part of his old face unaffected by the bug, the upper part of his left cheek, smooth human skin. Everything else was covered with blisters and burns and cuts and bleeds. Their fingers were swollen, fat sausages hanging off of their hands.

Any reasonable person would keep on running. Being in their presence, breathing their air, even being in the same building as someone who'd caught the bug was dangerous. But Vincent waited.

"You have to turn back," she said to the invaders. There were volumes contained in that sentence. It was one of her catch-phrases. Dr. Georgia Haskins was more than some random hero, she was a bell-weather, she embodied the fears and hopes and contradictions of everyone who lived inside the wall. She felt compassion for the people who'd caught the bug, compassion that was evident even now.

The barrier had to stay up, not because anyone wanted it to stay up, but because that was the way it had to be. That Dr. Haskins would steel her heart and go to work every day doing what she did, despite the pangs of her conscience, did not make her less of a person. It made her a hero.

Usually, they'd turn back. It was ambiguous whether they understood, on some level, that she was right and that they had no place here, or if they could tell she was willing pull the trigger. Or some combination of those two. The bottom line was, in the plays, they'd always turn around.

They came closer. "I told you to stop," Dr. Georgia Haskins said. At this point Vincent was already running.

He heard the noises her gun made as they surrounded her.

There was no cure. You had a year to live once you caught it, at best. They had nothing to gain from invading the cities. Popular opinion was that they were just pissed off.

Vincent made it to the helicopter, he got out of the city. He never told anybody about what he had seen that day, didn't put it in his book. It's one of the first things you learn in the business. People don't want to go backstage. Not really.

Humility

1

    Laura was walking home from a funeral when she saw the smoke rising up into the air. She had smelled it a moment earlier - the thought had crossed her mind that someone was burning leaves, or was barbecuing and had knocked over the grill, scattering lit charcoal on the grass. It was two o'clock in the afternoon, she'd have had this little street to herself even three years ago, but people were out of work, people were sitting on their front porches or their tiny front yards, walking from one end of the block talking to each other. The people on the street wore sweat pants and dirty T-shirts - the simple clothes they were still allowed to wear - and so did Laura. Laura lived in a house a block away from them, wore the same clothes that they did, expressed opinions similar to theirs on the scarce occasions when they talked to each other. And now Laura's house was on fire.

She was almost relieved. It'd happened. And it could have been much worse- she could have been at home.

She walked, breathed deeply but casually, tried not to look worried or concerned or excited. She pictured herself, a small person on a small planet circling the sun. She crossed the street at the intersection where she normally would have turned, passed the smoke cloud, imagined her few belongings melting or turning to ash, her microphone, her broadcasting equipment, her refrigerator. She didn't look, but she saw the spinning lights on top of the police cars. The cops were the only ones who had cars any more.

It was raining, drizzling. Not enough to put out the fire.

Now that the inevitable had happened, she had steps to follow, walking to do. She went to the market first. The idea was that wherever she happened to be, it would make sense for her to go to the market. Everybody went to the market. And once she was at the market, she could go anywhere.

You could see the Ferris wheel for miles around, it was easy to navigate to. She ducked into an alley just as the smell of corn dogs tickled her nose. The gravel was spread out unevenly, little islands of intact pavement sticking out here and there and a patch of grass touching the wall. A pair of stray cats were lying languidly by an empty dumpster. They watched as Laura took her clothes off, kneeled down by the green patch, and tore up the grass, grabbing a few strands at a time with the tips of her fingers and pulling, getting as much of the root as possible. Once enough of the grass was gone she started scooping up mud and spreading it on her skin. The rain was perfect, light enough to get the mud wet without washing it off. She rubbed it all over herself. She concealed as much of her face as she could; she shook her hair, messed it up, kneaded gravel into the weave.

Some of the penitents at least wore underwear, but Laura saw no reason not to go all the way. She dumped her clothes and her shoes into the dumpster, went deeper into the alley, found a sewer grate, and pushed her wallet through. It fell and she never heard it splash.

She continued towards the market. There was a long line of people waiting at the booth just outside the fence. They checked each person's ID card. Hypothetically, no one was supposed to go to the market more than three or four times a month, a small release. In practice you could go every night of the week, as long as whatever happened at the market stayed there. The teenagers in the dark red uniforms and the machine-guns let her walk into the market without looking at her too closely. She saw other women dressed the same way that she was, yelling at people or staring or walking around holding signs.

Laura circled the market. There were men wearing suits and women wearing make-up and gold tiaras, music playing from junkyard sound systems and the same men and women dancing lewdly, elaborate meals being served on folding outdoor tables on fine china, wine glasses, silk tableclothes. There were people who almost lived here, who took other names and did everything they could to forget about the world outside.

She made the rounds for an hour and left through the gate opposite the one by which she'd arrived. As long as the ferris wheel was directly behind her, she knew she was moving north. There was no one around, no reason to be clever now. The later it got, the smaller the chance that anyone she came across would see an untouchable penitent and the more likely that they'd just see a naked, unarmed woman. She ran.

Pebbles dug into the bottoms of her feet and she ignored them. No more houses now - train tracks, steel doorways, giant faceless buildings.

She headed down an alley and knocked on a rusted metal fire door. Two long, four short. She thought about covering herself but decided not to worry about it. She was naked, she just was. They were going to have to deal with it.

She waited. Nothing happened. There was no point in knocking again.

Someone came up behind her; by the time she noticed their presence there was a wet rag in her face, chemical smell, sleep.

2

She woke up in a dark room. She was wearing clothes, which was nice, and was lying on the floor, which was fine. She sat up.

She collected herself before she said anything, thought carefully.

"I'm awake."

She heard whispering and turned so that she was facing the door as it opened. A man stepped in and a lightbulb overhead came to life. The room was an empty walk-in closet. The walls were white drywall; mold grew in the corners.

The man was wearing a black leather jacket with useless little metal spikes all over it that he clearly took very good care of. The style was very similar to the people at the market, although he would probably never admit that - save up to buy one beautiful thing and show it off like a peacock in mating season.

"You knew the knock," the man said.

"Do you recognize the sound of my voice?"

He didn't respond, she decided that meant yes.

"I was contacted by the group here a year ago. I was told that if I had to get out of the city quickly a door would be open for me."

"Who contacted you?"

"Sparrow."

"That was a year ago. You never checked to see if the door was still open."

Stupid question, patronizing and insulting, maybe deliberately.

"There's no safe way to check. Not without putting you at risk."

"Contacting you in the first place put us at risk." He got up and started pacing back and forth. Showing off his shiny jacket.

"Why did Sparrow contact you? What was in it for him?"

"I assumed that he listened to me on the radio and agreed with what I had to say. I don't have anything to offer you."

"No shit." He paused, then kept talking. "My understanding is that you're religious, that that's what your radio broadcasts were about. Are you really a penitent?"

"No. I disguised myself to get into the market. No one followed me."

"Did you enjoy that? Walking naked through the crowd?"

Hair raising on the back of her neck. This was not right. Her expression didn't change. "It was the safest way."

"I doubt that it felt safe. I doubt that you feel safe now." He turned towards her suddenly. "Sparrow hasn't been in charge for a few months now. Our philosophy has changed. We're less political, more practical. And we were never religious. I don't know why Sparrow thought it was important that you held up one book written by dead people while the other side holds up a book written by another dead person but it has nothing to do with our cause."

"I don't know anything about that. I was told there was a safe way out of the city that I could take advantage of. That's all I knew."

"And you believed what you were told?"

"I had a source who corroborated what Sparrow said. But she's not with us anymore."

"I'm sure your philosophy was a consolation to her when they set her house on fire."

That hurt. He kept talking.

"The bottom line is that you don't appear to have anything to pay your way with. If you weren't a pacifist we could at least find you something useful to do."

I'm not a pacifist. She didn't say it out loud, didn't feel like explaining it. Looking at him, looking at her now, she was convinced that he'd been there when they taken her in, naked and covered in mud. He hadn't laid a hand on her himself, she was sure of that, but he'd watched, and he'd silently rehearsed this conversation many times.

She leaned back on the palms of her hand, looked him in the eye and spoke.

"I think we both know where this is going."

She glanced at the doorway.

"I'm sure there must be somewhere more comfortable then here."

He stayed where he was long enough to make her wonder if she'd miscalculated. Then he smiled, a satisfied shit-eating grin.

"Yeah. Follow me."

He opened the door. There was another man standing right outside the doorway, taller then the first, a weightlifter, his torso an inverted triangle. He was wearing a hat with a tall green feather. He exchanged a nod with the man with the leather jacket and let them pass. The man in the leather jacket walked and Laura followed.

They were in what appeared to be a floor of an old office building. There was a thick layer of dust covering the dark blue carpet; there were visible footprints going in both directions. The man in the black leather jacket was focused on a closed door at the end of the hall. As they approached the room, they passed another doorway. She heard voices inside, quiet, nervous arguments. She saw maps hanging on the walls out of the corner of her eye. This was the work room.

She went into the work room. Smoothly, like a train switching tracks. She looked around. There were a few of them, sequestered away in cubicles. They each had one small piece of flair in defiance of humility - a hat, a piece of jewelry, something that shone or sparkled or popped.

"I'm sure some of you recognize my voice," she said. "I came here because I've been targeted and was told this place would be safe."

They stopped what they were doing. She had no way to tell who they were, how long they'd been here, how many of them had come in under Sparrow and how many were only familiar with the new leader.

"This man is planning to rape me. He allowed me to see his face first, which means he probably doesn't plan on letting me live."

The man in the black leather jacket came running into the room. He opened his mouth. Laura stared at him.

She felt their eyes looking her over. She didn't move.

I am a small person on a small planet, hurtling through infinite space.

3

The gave her papers, clothing that fit her cover, and a train ticket. Her story was that she was taking her pilgrimage. She wore a plain black dress, which technically fell within the bounds of the law. Simplicity looked very different depending on how much money you had, or were supposed to have.

She'd seen their faces and they'd let her go. The only thing she could do to pay back their trust was do everything in her power to not get caught. No more radio for her, not for a very long time.

She didn't know what they were going to do to Sparrow. She didn't need to know.

There was a group of penitents standing at the platform. They stared at the train as it left the station.

Super Jesus

1

Father John was in the process of eating a Cinnabun when he received a vision. He was sitting in the food court of the mall near the house he rented a room in when the vision came to him. His first thought was that the vision might just be a man in an unusual costume approaching him at an unusual time, but he quickly noticed that none of the other people sitting at the food court seemed to notice or acknowledge the man who had appeared before him. Also, the man in question appeared to be floating several feet above the ground. Father John tried hard to keep realistic possibilities in mind for why this might be happening. He'd seen magicians perform tricks like this on television, and once in person when he was twelve and his grandmother had taken him to Las Vegas. But he didn't see any props or any place to conceal them, and when he looked at the space between the top of the man's head and the vaulted ceiling of the shopping center he didn't see any kind of rope, cord, or thread that might be supporting him.

There was still a possibility, and John knew he was reaching now, that the man was some kind of hologram, or that he was using some kind of advanced technology to levitate in the air. Father John had read a lot of science fiction novels as a teenager. He'd seen Star Trek, and watched programs on cable that showed some of the amazing things that were being developed by the military or in private laboratories. So there was a distant possibility that there was a reasonable explanation for what he was seeing.

But Father John doubted it.

The man floating several feet above the ground in front of Father John was wearing a green super-bunny costume. Father John was one of about a dozen people walking the face of the earth who could identify a super-bunny costume on sight. The super-bunny was his invention - at the age of six, when his mother had asked him what he'd like to be for Halloween, he'd immediately answered, without any further prompting or input of any kind, that he wanted to be a green super-bunny. His mother had thought that was funny, and so she made him a green costume with bunny ears and a cape and an orange felt B across his chest. There were still pictures of him wearing this costume at his parents' home.

The costume Father John was looking at now was different in several ways than the one he had worn as a child. It was larger; the man floating in the air in front of him was at least six feet tall and heavily built, and his costume clung tightly to his skin, revealing the definition of his abs, biceps, and thighs in the manner of modern super-hero comic book art. Also, the felt B that Father John had worn on his version of the costume had been replaced by a giant neon purple J, which seemed to gently emit light from the floating man's chest.

The man's skin, which was only visible in the area of his face, was dark green, and seamlessly matched the color of his costume. His lips were pink, as was his tongue, which only became visible when he began to speak.

"Good afternoon, Father John. I am Super Jesus." The man's voice was deep and sincere and masculine, and reminded John of Forties' radio serials.

Father John didn't answer the floating man. Privately, he was deeply concerned that he might be going insane, and was trying to remember the details of the conversation he and his classmates had taken part in with one of his older and wiser professors about how a person could distinguish a hallucination from a communication from God. It hadn't been that long ago - John was a recent graduate of the seminary, and was still in the process of finding a church in which to practice ministry - but in the heat of the moment he could not remember the critical details of the talk.

Outwardly, John was attempting to put on a good pastor face. Caring, strong, peaceful, confident, simultaneously accepting and distant.

The floating man hesitated. He didn't seem certain how to proceed. Finally deciding on a direct approach, he took a deep breath and cleared his throat.

"I want you to go out and kill some prostitutes, John."

He waited for an answer from John, but did not receive one. John's pastor face had frozen into a stationary mask, and he seemed unable to move.

"With an axe," Super Jesus added, hoping that might help.

Father John got up and left the mall, leaving the remains of his cinnamon roll where they were on the table.

2

Over the course of the next few days, Super Jesus was a constant presence in John's life and perceptions. Wherever John went, Super Jesus went also, floating in front, below, or above him. He talked constantly; he had a few modes of speech, between which he alternated every few hours. He would quote long bible passages, then he would switch and sound like Adam West trying to recruit someone to join the Air Force. And then he would just start begging, repetitively.

"Why can't you just do it? Come on! It wouldn't even be that hard. Come on! Why can't you just do it?"

John walked through the park, watching the ducklings fight over bread crumbs. He was lucky that he was having this problem now. He'd already decided to take a couple of weeks off to read and relax before he really started hunting for jobs. He hadn't planned to spend that time fighting for his sanity, but he knew he could disappear for a few days and no one would suspect anything unusual was happening.

He'd decided that he would seek outside spiritual and psychiatric help at the first sign that his resolve might be slipping, but he was doing fine so far. He had not replied to Super Jesus or acknowledged his presence, not once. He had bought an axe at a hardware store, but as Super Jesus had pointed out, an axe was just a useful thing to own, and purchasing one didn't necessarily obligate a person to any particular course of action. You never knew when you might want to chop down a tree, or hack away at a stubborn bush root, or do something else that you needed an axe for. He knew that Super Jesus was a hallucination, but that didn't mean that the things he said were necessarily incorrect. It was important that he be logical and unbiased if he was going to get past this.

That Tuesday evening, the woman in whose house John rented a room was holding her book club. The book club was mostly an excuse to get drunk; the club was going to be down there all night talking, and there was no way John was going to get any sleep if he stayed in the house. So, at Super Jesus' suggestion, he got a hotel room. Over the course of his seminary training, he had spent a short period of time doing street ministry in a blighted neighborhood, and he knew that getting a room in that area would be far less expensive than going to a hotel elsewhere, so that was where he went. He brought the axe with him.

Sitting on the bed in his room, holding his new axe, he was overwhelmed by the noise all around him. The walls seemed to be made of tissue paper; he could hear people fighting and yelling and having sex in the other rooms. Outside his window, traffic rushed by and police sirens wailed. At least once he heard a gun being fired.

It took him a while to notice that Super Jesus was no longer with him. He was free - he'd faced his crisis and come through the other side unscathed. He could now act freely, safe in the knowledge that he was making his own decisions.

He knew it would be a bad idea for him to enlist the services of a prostitute, that it was not only morally wrong but deeply unwise given the circumstances. He did it anyway. Everyone has moments like that, John later reflected. You know that candy bars make people fat. You know that you yourself are not exempt from this rule. You know it's more important to you to not be fat than it is to enjoy the taste of chocolate. You eat the candy bar anyway.

He knew he shouldn't get the hooker. He went out and got the hooker.

It didn't take long, he just walked up and down the street and waited to be approached. She claimed that her name was Becky. She had curly red hair and had an unbelievably, disturbingly youthful appearance, like a high school student fresh out of gymnastics practice. The tattoo on the back of her hand and the scar running from under her left ear down her neck to her shoulder were collectively unable to alter this impression - they didn't fit the rest of the picture, and John ignored them without even having to try. She was wearing high heels and black fishnets, and had big brown eyes.

John held the door to his room open for her and she went inside. At some point in the process of hiring Becky and bringing her back to the hotel room, Super Jesus had returned. He hadn't said a word - he was just staring at Becky. The expression on his face would have been appropriate on a child's face on Christmas morning.

Becky saw the axe, leaning against the wall near the nightstand. She took a step backwards.

"No."

She left the room as quickly as she could, shaking her head and muttering to herself as she did it.

"No. No fucking way."

She went down the hall, moving as quickly as she could in her heels back towards the hotel parking lot.

3

John followed Becky out into the hallway but didn't get much further than the doorway to his room. He stood there and watched her go.

"Well, that's great," Super Jesus said. "That's fantastic." The voice Super Jesus had adopted was similar to his own, the unfamiliar version of himself he heard on other people's answering machines. "Fantastic. Way to go."

At this point John turned around, looked Super Jesus in the eye, and spoke to him, hissing through his teeth at the end of each sentence.

"I shouldn't be doing this anyway." Hiss. "This is wrong." Hiss. Huff and puff. "I'm a man of God now." Hiss.

Super Jesus was about to fire back when they were both surprised by the sound of a man laughing. They turned as one in the direction of the noise and saw an elderly man in a plain white T-shirt and grey sweat pants. His thin hair was stark white and he had a bright red alcoholic's nose that had obviously been broken more than once. He was overweight.

"Couldn't get it up, couldja?" The man chuckled and awkwardly shifted his weight onto his left foot, nearly falling over in the process. "I've been there. Fucking hookers, man."

John had a complicated relationship to his own sexuality. The idea that he'd entered the seminary to avoid women was silly - he wasn't Catholic, after all, the common punch line to many seminary jokes- but he hadn't had much in the way of relationships and had only had sex twice, both under circumstances he'd just as soon forget.

It didn't usually bother him when people made fun of him, even about something as personal as the possibility of his impotence. He wasn't sure why he was so upset now. It had something to do with the man's tone, it was like he was really trying to be friends. It touched him somewhere deep, reminding him of classmates in elementary school who would be nice one day and bully him the next.

"Fuck you," he whispered, spitting it out and losing commitment toward the end. He turned away, embarrassed now. When he glanced up he saw the fat man walking towards him, angrily shaking his finger, the righteous common man confronting the politician. He resembled Santa Claus even more than he had before.

Super Jesus had vanished.

John went back into his hotel room. He re-emerged from the room with the axe at almost exactly the same moment that the fat man reached him. Calmly, letting gravity do the work, he swung the axe with both hands, down and forward into the drunken man's chest. It cut into his heart with a loud, wet, healthy sound, splattering John's shirt and face with the fat man's blood.

John took a step backwards and to the side, leaving the axe lodged in the man's chest. The man's weight was such that he leaned back on his heels, was still for a moment, and then fell forward, into the hotel room. John poked his nose out into the hallway and did a quick look in both directions. He didn't see anybody - as far as he could tell, there were no witnesses.

There was remarkably little blood in the hallway, just a few drops that had somehow made it from the wound in the man's chest down to the carpet before he fell forward. John moved the welcome mat that had been in front of his door into the middle of the hallway, so that it covered the stain.

He closed the door. There was blood spilling out from under the man's face-down body, but the poor construction of the motel was working in his favor and the blood was flowing away from the doorway, where it was in any case being quickly soaked up by the thick orange carpet.

The room smelled like rust. The people next door were continuing to have loud, violent sex.

John sat down on the foot of the bed and thought.

Dave would help him. He called Dave using the phone in his room. Dave was an old friend of John's from high school who he didn't actually see that much anymore, but there was no doubt in his mind that Dave would be willing to help him out. They had the kind of friendship that didn't seem to be affected by time - no matter how long it had been, whenever they got back in touch it was like they were still in the cafeteria of their high school, talking about philosophy. Dave had been a Satanist for a while, but he'd given it up shortly before graduation. He was a Unitarian minister now. He'd gotten started a little sooner than John had.

Dave answered. He sounded sleepy. John begged him to come to the hotel. Dave was confused, but John was Dave's friend. He promised that he'd be right down.

A half an hour later, someone knocked on the door of the hotel room. John looked through the peephole. It was Dave. John let Dave into the room.

Dave looked down at the fat man's body. His jaw dropped and he did not move.

"I know it's a lot to wrap your mind around," John said. "Let me explain."

John told Dave about Super Jesus. He started from the beginning and included all the important details. It took a long time for Dave to understand what John was trying to say.

"So…" Dave blinked a lot. "…so this man…"

"Super Jesus," John corrected him.

Dave took a deep breath. "Super Jesus," he said. "Super Jesus wanted you to kill this person."

"No," John said, shaking his head furiously. "Super Jesus was just in the room when I did it." Super Jesus was back in the room now, listening to everything taking place, looking concerned, like a pediatrician evaluating a set of symptoms and not wanting to interrupt.

"John, you need help. We should call somebody."

Super Jesus shook his head sadly. He pointed at Dave and then dragged his finger across his own throat.

4

Ten minutes later there was a knock on the door of the hotel room. John looked through the peephole and saw an elderly woman wearing a polo shirt with the logo of the motel on it.

He yelled through the door, he didn't open it.

"Hello?"

"Sir, there have been complaints about the noise."

"All right, I'm sorry, we'll keep it down," he yelled.

"Sir, could you please open the door?"

John had Dave's body lying on the bed next to the fat man's. He'd been in the process of wrapping sheets around them when he'd been interrupted. The carpet was still soaked in blood, as was John's face and his clothes, which he'd taken off and thrown into the bathtub.

"Look, I'm sorry, but I promise everything will be fine…"

"Sir, I need to open the door."

John attempted to summon his pastor voice.

"With all due respect, ma'am, there are half a dozen people here making more noise than I am and those are just the ones I can hear from my room."

John's pastor voice had no effect whatsoever.

"I don't need you to tell me how to do my job. Open the door."

"She's an innocent person," Super Jesus said sadly. "She's just doing her job." He assumed an exaggerated thinking pose, going down on one knee and resting his chin on his fist. "Although it's not impossible that she used to be a prostitute… she might even moonlight as a prostitute. Some men like that." Sounding like Adam West again. "There are sick and disgusting people in the world, John."

John opened the door. John would later have time to reflect on the fact that her eyes were drawn immediately to his penis, rather than to the blood covering his face.

"What in the name of God's green earth…"

He grabbed her, pulled her into the room, and slammed the door shut.

Rather then using the ax, he strangled her, which was not very hard because she was old and infirm. He killed her this way, rather than using the ax, because he wanted to avoid getting blood on her clothes, but after he was finished and stripped her clothes off he found that, in the process of pinning her to the bloody carpet, he'd stained her clothes anyway. Her shirt was covered with red spots and was useless now, but her pants had already been dark in color and the blood wasn't really noticeable unless you were looking closely. He removed the woman's pants, rinsed them out in the bathtub, and hung them over the shower curtain.

While the pants dried, he thought about what he should do. Super Jesus wasn't offering any advice, he was just standing there in the middle of the room looking judgmental. In order to figure out what to do, he decided to list his immediate problems. He had three bodies to get rid of, and a hotel room that was covered in blood. That was it. Not so bad, really. He could deal with everything else later.

The people in the next room were still having hard, rhythmic, furniture-shaking sex.

He decided to move the bodies to his car. He didn't have enough sheets to wrap around all three bodies and successfully conceal them. He waited for a while, until the pants were dry, and put them on. They were a tight fit but he made them work. He left the room, wearing nothing but the pants, and walked up and down the hall until he found a doorway with a broken lock. He pushed the door open and looked inside the room. It was empty except for a maid's cleaning cart. He took a white bag full of dirty sheets and a bottle of bleach from the cart, thought about it for a moment, then put everything back onto the cart and just wheeled the whole thing back to his own room.

He wrapped each of the three bodies in sheets until he ran out of sheets. By the time he was done the three bodies definitely still looked like three bodies wrapped in white sheets, but at least there was no blood. He spent the next few hours covering the mattress and the carpet in bleach and trying to get rid of the blood stains.

He mostly succeeded, but it took a long time. The sun was rising by the time he finished. Using the maid cart, he made four trips between his car and the motel room, transporting a body the first three times and bringing over a pile of bloody sheets and clothing on the fourth. The first body made it to the trunk of the car without incident; blood started soaking through the sheets of the second body when he was halfway across the parking lot, but there was nobody there to notice.

As he crammed the last of the three bodies into the trunk, a minivan pulled up next to his car and a large family began to unload, a mom and a dad and lots and lots of children, each of whom seemed to own a Game Boy.

As the family patriarch climbed down from the driver's side of the minivan and followed his children into the parking lot, John pushed down hard on the last body, in order to get it to fit in the trunk. As he pushed, a red plume emerged from inside the dirty white wrapping, suddenly bringing the blood to the surface and again staining his hands.

The father was in the process of yelling something to his kids when he glanced to the side and saw the bloody mess in John's trunk. He looked at John, John looked at him; their eyes met. John still wasn't wearing anything except for the old woman's pants.

The man pointedly turned away and followed his children into the parking lot.

"Okay kids, first person to the room gets TV control for the night…"

John slammed the trunk shut, got behind the wheel, and drove away.

5

John got away. He went back to the house where his room was. He didn't know what he was going to do with the bodies in the trunk. He ended up leaving them where they were and just parking his car in out of the way places, moving it frequently so that no one noticed the smell. He knew it was a bad idea, and that he needed to find a more permanent solution, but he found that he had a deep aversion to opening the trunk. As long as the trunk was closed, he didn't have to admit that anything unusual had happened, or that he had done anything wrong. He remembered the murders he had committed only hazily, as though they were something that had happened in a dream, or as though the fact that they had taken place was the subject of an article he'd skimmed in a magazine last month.

He did not see Super Jesus in the days following the murders. The morning after, it did briefly seem as though his landlady had grown green bunny ears, but he was able to make the hallucination go away by concentrating. He was happy about this, he was in control again. Aside from the bodies in the trunk of his car, he had nothing to worry about.

His mentor from the seminary called him that Thursday with good news. A church wanted him to fill in for a Sunday, the pastor had to leave town at the last moment. The pastor was old, he might be looking to retire soon. They were giving him a test drive. This was a big deal.

John threw himself into writing a sermon for that Sunday. It occupied all of his attention - all of his other problems faded from view. He was sure to get plenty of sleep the night before and eat a big breakfast that morning. The church was about an hour's drive away, and far from any train station or bus stop, as tended to be the case out in the suburbs. He really had no choice except to drive the car that still had the bodies in it. He looked up a map of the church on the internet the night before and found an isolated place he could park, a lot in the middle of a nearby park. He'd put the car there, walk over to the church, do his sermon, drink some coffee and schmooze, and come back. No problem.

He went over the sermon in his mind over and over again as he drove to the church on Sunday morning. The anticipation gave him a lead foot. At the time that he saw the spinning lights in his rear-view mirror, he had not had cause to think about the contents of his trunk all morning.

He pulled over. He suddenly saw green bunnies everywhere. The sky turned green. As one of the two police officers got out of the car (she was young, had her blonde hair pulled back in a ponytail, and was rather astoundingly attractive for a cop) he briefly imagined her with a little bright green bushy tail. But he focused, and the world returned to normal. This was going to be all right.

The pretty blonde cop stopped walking on her way to the driver's side. She sniffed, and looked down at the trunk.

"Look at her," Super Jesus said. He was sitting in the back seat. "Look at how she walks. I think we both know what this means."

John put the car in gear and stomped on the gas pedal. Super Jesus laughed maniacally.

He got away. He was very lucky. He'd been driving through a forest preserve, the roads curved a lot and there was a major fork not far from where he'd been pulled over. He went left. As far as he could tell the police that stopped him must have gone right.

He made it to the parking lot. It was empty; it was full of weeds, the trees around it were overgrown. He parked the car and went into the woods. Not long afterward, he heard sirens and people shouting.

He made it to the church a few minutes late, he was going in the wrong direction when he looked up and saw the steeple peeking up over the tree line. There were some giant interconnected pieces of plastic in the backyard of the church with children crawling on them. The kids all stopped and stared at John as he walked around to the front of the church.

He went inside, went to the front of the church. People were still taking their seats. He turned on the microphone and started talking.

In back of the church were a pair of teenagers with an expensive camcorder. They also had a digital recorder plugged into the sound system of the church. They were members of the church's youth group, recording the sermon was part of a school project they were completing. Neither of them would do anything to embarrass the church, but the recording they made would later be stolen by one of their siblings and wind up on the internet.

"I had another sermon prepared today," John said. "But instead, I'd like to talk to you about Super Jesus.

"Super Jesus is green. Although I've never seen him move anything, he's very large and probably very strong. Super Jesus talks with a lot of authority. The things he says usually make a lot of sense.

"I don't know what it is with Super Jesus and prostitutes..."

He talked for about half an hour before the cops showed up.

Red Rover

1

The trip back home had put him in a mood to go somewhere, anywhere where something was going on, and to do it tonight, before his time was up and he found himself looking back on a month's worth of sleeping in and watching television. There was an ad for an amateur theater group in the free local newspaper, and that evening he found himself driving to where they'd be performing.

The main line of stores disappeared as he traveled; it was echoed by a block of strip malls and minor industry, which were followed by a group of parks, and then by houses. Winter was late in coming this year - the grass was dead, but there was no snow to cover it. The trees around him got taller as the road narrowed; for a moment he felt like he was going through a tunnel. Then they disappeared, revealing a line of brick storefronts and old-fashioned streetlights on brass poles.

He had an hour to kill before the play started. He parked his car.

There was an ice cream shop on the corner. A bank of freezers was laid out along the back wall and a row of chalkboards above them listed the flavors they each contained. A kid with long red hair had his head down on the counter next to the cash register. His eyes were closed. Ryan walked over to him, waited for a minute, and knocked twice, loudly, on the register's metal shell. The kid opened his eyes and stood up.

"I'd like a vanilla ice cream cone," Ryan said.

Ryan paid for his ice cream and took a seat facing the front window. A girl was sitting three chairs down from him. She was wearing a purple sweater and a pair of black sweat pants, and had a mass of brown hair pouring down from the top of her head, covering most of her face. Her body was shapeless, like a giant toddler's. He only knew she was a girl because of the knitting needles in her hands. She was making something out of orange yarn.

She saw him and looked him in the eye. He found himself wondering about her gender again. He could see her face now- her left eye was a little lower than her right, and her chin was skewed to one side. He continued to think of her as a girl. She made him nervous, eager not to say the wrong thing.

"You have really strong arms," she said, stopping her knitting. She emphasized the word strong, as though she were comparing his arms to something else on account of their strength. Emily had said the same thing; it was the first thing she'd ever said to him.

The day he arrived at school, he saw her walking down the sidewalk, carrying a huge suitcase and having some trouble with it. He offered to help. That was when she'd said it. Ryan was huge, seven feet tall and wider then a refrigerator, while Emily was a twig; she had brown hair going down to her waist, and when Ryan first saw her, he was afraid that she'd be carried away by the wind, like a kite.

They were a couple inside of a month. People thought it was hysterical, the two of them walking down the street, her hand buried inside his. They kept making jokes about it even after Emily told him she didn't want him around any more; they weren't being mean, they just hadn't heard. It took a week or so for the news to get around

"Thanks," Ryan said, the polite thing to say to anyone. He sampled his ice cream, gave himself a chance to think. "What are you making?"

She smiled at him, put her sewing needles down onto the table in front of her, and opened her hands. Suspended from her fingertips was an intricate web, thickly woven around the edges but hollow in the center.

"That's very pretty," Ryan said. He was angry with himself the moment the words left his mouth. He was being patronizing. It was much better then pretty.

"Thank you. But look." She picked up one of her knitting needles, and twisted her hand around so that it blocked his view of the yarn. She slid the needle into the web and straightened her wrist so that Ryan could see it clearly again. The needle had vanished.

"Nice trick," he said.

She just smiled and straightened her fingers, stretching and attenuating the strands of the web until he was sure that one of them was going to snap. He watched, carefully, waiting for the moment to come.

And the web vanished. When he looked back up, the girl was gone too. The second of the two knitting needles was still lying on the table.

Ryan got up and walked towards the counter.

"Excuse me, did you see where the person I was talking to just went?"

"You're the only person here."

"I am now. There was a girl in here a second ago."

"There haven't been any customers in here in the last hour, except you. I'm closing up in a minute, you're going to have to leave."

"She was right there."

"Whatever you say. Don't forget that thing you brought in with you." He pointed at the needle.

Ryan felt himself getting angry. He was about to raise his voice when something buckled under his fingertips and he found himself with a small piece of plywood in his hand. He froze. The plywood had come from a long supporting strip under the counter. He had been tightening his grip on it, not noticing what he was doing.

He let the piece of wood fall into his pocket, struggling not to break eye contact with the cashier as he did it.

"Fine," he whispered. He walked over to the table by the window, picked up the knitting needle, and left the shop.

He looked down at his hand as he walked away. He'd been getting better, but he still got mad sometimes.

Night fell as he approached his destination. The community center was a rectangular, bright red brick building, taller than it was wide. Thick hedges bordered the lot the center had been built on, setting it apart from the surrounding houses. A narrow passageway led to a parking lot in back; the spaces were empty except for a big white bus that had the logo of a nearby retirement community on the side of it. A set of concrete steps was sitting against the rear wall, leading up to a thick metal door.

Inside, there was a low office ceiling, a dark blue linoleum floor, and a pair of hallways branching off in separate directions. The walls were covered with bulletin boards, crayon drawings, notices for future events, fliers, newspaper clippings, photographs.

In the middle of the open area where the hallways intersected was a traffic barrier with a piece of poster-board attached to it. It was a sign, spelling out the name of the play, a pencil drawing which had been painted over with brightly colored stripes. They stretched from the top edge of the poster-board to the bottom, and were all nearly vertical.

To the right was a bank of fire doors- their windows had been covered up from the inside by layers of old newspaper. Ryan's ribs brushed against the metal frame of the doorway as he slipped inside.

On either side of the entrance were two portable spotlights, pointing towards the stage. The auditorium was filled with folding chairs, but only the front row was occupied. Ryan took a look at the people sitting up there; he could see white hair in the places where the spotlights grazed the top of their heads. He sat down in the chair closest to him.

A dozen streaks of color had been directed towards the ceiling, several long strips of fabric, tied to the rafters and tethered to the boards, each one slightly wider than Ryan's shoulders. Together they formed a back wall into and from which the actors onstage could appear and vanish. Her clothing was made of the same material, and its colors had been cut to match their background perfectly. Her blonde hair and pale skin blended with the yellow streamer that cut across her shoulders. Standing still in the dim lighting, she was completely hidden. He only saw her when she blinked. She had bright blue eyes.

Ryan hadn't spoken with Abbie in a little over two years, and he'd taken it for granted that he would never see her again. They'd known each other in high school, but had never had an extended conversation. He had only touched her only once, on the shoulder, to get her attention.

The spotlights hovered in place. They began to overlap as they expanded, and by the time everything was lit up, the line dividing them had entirely disappeared. Ryan looked over his shoulder- there were two large men operating the lights whose faces Ryan could not quite make out through the glare. Onstage, three actors stepped out from behind the curtain. They wore bright red silk clothing, had short black hair, and were barefoot. Their feet were dirty white, like a storm cloud, and so were their faces. Ryan wondered how much make-up they had on, how much trouble it had been to apply. He began to wonder how much effort had been put into all this.

One of the actors stepped forward. He spoke, and his words were somehow amplified, filling the auditorium.

"Red Rover, Act One."

He stepped back. Abbie was still standing there behind them, still motionless, but now visible in the bright light. Her eyes were still closed.

The three actors began to walk in circles, passing just behind the curtain of silk on one end and straddling the edge of the stage with their feet on the other. They were mumbling under their breath; Ryan couldn't tell what they were saying. A minute and a half rolled by. Jason began to wonder if the play had started, or if this was meant to give people a chance to get into their seats.

Abbie stepped away from the curtain, and her clothing fell suddenly out of sync with the streamers behind her. Her head was down, and her back was hunched over, as though she were hiding behind something. She was watching the three actors intently. They didn't seem to notice that she was there, but as one of them brushed up against the silk curtain, a green apple somehow appeared in his hands. Its awkward natural color stood violently in contrast with the sharp primaries and secondaries of everything else onstage.

She raised her head. The three actors stopped in their tracks and their heads snapped in her direction.

She sprinted to the far side of the stage, right through them, her eyes wide open in panic, and swung her hands out into the air as though she were trying to grab a hold of something. The actors walked slowly in her direction; she turned around and ran again, but this time, as she passed between the three men, she fell to the ground.

The actor with the apple approached her, and the other two actors followed behind him. They formed a triangle pointing in her direction.

After a moment of hesitation, Abbie rose up, onto her knees, her eyes closed and her mouth hanging slightly open. The leader handed her the apple, and she took a bite.

Abbie had been very badly allergic to apples in high school. Ryan remembered a time when she had eaten a piece of sour candy, thinking that the apple flavor was artificial. She didn't finish school that day, and wasn't able to come back for two weeks.

After three bites, her body started shaking. She kept eating. When there was nothing left to gnaw on, the apple core fell from her fingers, and she collapsed.

The people in the front row rose up as one, whispering unhappily. They filed towards the center aisle, temporarily blocking Ryan's view, and left the auditorium. Abbie was still shaking. She would start, stop, and start again, in regular intervals.

Ryan stood up. He felt a hand come to rest on his shoulder. He turned around, and saw one of the men who'd been operating the spotlights standing in the aisle between him and the exit. The man took Ryan's hand, and slid something soft and insubstantial into his palm. Ryan looked at it closely. It was a lock of hair, long brown hair. Emily's hair.

"Where did you get this?"

The man's face was still concealed by the bright light behind him.

"What did you do to her?"

Again, there was no answer - he just stood there.

He got angry again. The muscles in his hands contracted into fists. He punched the man in the face. The man stumbled backwards, knocking over one of the spotlights. It hit the ground, and the sound of its bulb shattering echoed throughout the auditorium. Ryan charged. They ploughed through the fire doors into the hallway outside.

They hit the ground. Ryan was on top. He was nearly blinded by the light. He hit the man again and again.

"Where is…"

Before he could finish, the second spotlight operator grabbed him from behind. A pair of arms wrapped around his body, pinning his right arm against his ribs, and something sharp dug into his shoulder. He reached back and clawed at the man's face with his free hand, kicked frantically, somehow got to his feet.

When he stepped away he saw the two men, clearly for the first

time. They were as tall as he was, built like bulldogs, with huge shoulders and absent necks. They were wrapped from head to toe with black gauze, with only single narrow opening for their
mouths. Around the edges of those openings Ryan could see their skin - it was cracked, blistered, discolored like molded cheese. They had wide mouths, filled with tiny white triangles.

Ryan touched his shoulder. It didn't hurt that much, but there was lots of blood. His clothes were stained, and part of his shirt had been torn off.

The thing ran at him again, leading with its chin. As it approached, Ryan reached out, grabbed the top of its head, and pulled it past himself, hard, driving it head first into the wall. Before the second one could do anything, Ryan ran towards it, wrapped his arm around its neck, and squeezed.

"Where is she?" Nothing; it didn't even gasp for air. Ryan tightened his grip, to no effect. The first monster backed away from the wall and ran towards him in exactly the same way, chin first. Ryan dragged the creature he was choking out of the way and kicked the charger in the kneecap. It fell to the ground clutching its leg.

The monster in his arms stopped moving, and ceased to support its own weight. Ryan pushed it to the side, and kicked its partner in the head with the side of his foot. It shook its head back and forth, confused.

He kicked it again, and again and again. His leg was like a piston. He didn't stop until the sweat had gotten into his eyes and the room started spinning around him. He looked at the thing's face. Its eyes were closed, and most of its teeth were broken. The thing suddenly sprung up, fast like a mousetrap, and Ryan kicked again, without thinking. His heel landed squarely on the creature's windpipe. He felt something crack.

Ryan stepped away, glanced down at the bodies on the floor, felt a dark cloud spread from the back of his head towards his eyelids.

In the center of the stage, half-concealed in the absence of the second spotlight, was a wooden box, the size of a coffin. Abbie was not in sight, and neither were two of the actors. The third was standing behind the box. His right arm was concealed by the darkness; in his left was a long curved sword. Its metal surface shone like a mirror.

Ryan ran towards him.

He woke up. He was lying face up on a hard wooden floor. He

looked around without moving his head. Faint traces of light snuck in through the cracks of the floorboards above him. The pieces of the wall he'd crashed through were lying all around him.

The two monsters were sitting on the floor with their legs folded. They had emptied Ryan's pockets. One of them was holding his wallet and key chain; the other was looking at the piece of wood he had broken off of the counter at the ice-cream shop.

Ryan shifted his weight, slowly, trying to remain unnoticed. He felt the knitting needle press against his body from inside his jacket pocket. He glanced back up at the hole near the ceiling, and when he looked back down, one of monsters was glaring at him. He didn't even think. He pulled the needle out of his jacket and thrust it into the creature's neck.

It slipped through the creature's body like wet tissue paper. When he pulled it back, the monster's head and neck had been severed and warped, as though by a great heat. The second monster dropped the wallet. Ryan stabbed it through the heart, and it collapsed into a puddle on the floor.

Ryan pulled himself up through the hole near the ceiling, emerging at the foot of the stage. The actors were lined up in a row behind the box. Running through it at different angles were half a dozen swords, identical to the one Ryan had seen before.
They didn't even seem to notice Ryan until he climbed onstage with the needle in his hand. They saw him and stepped back, looked at him, looked at each other. They were confused. This wasn't supposed to happen.

Ryan ran towards them, screaming, his fingers locked into place by the cold.

2

He was woken up by daylight. He got up and took a look at his shoulder. He was unharmed; his shirt was still torn, but the blood stains had vanished. The sewing needle was gone.

The folding chairs were exactly where they had been before. The silk streamers were gone. The spotlight he had knocked over was gone too, but the other one was still right where it had been.

The box was still there. He reached down, and swung the lid open on its hinges. There was nothing inside.

He remembered - it had handed him her hair before he'd approached the stage. He'd had it in his hand when he'd left the theater.

He approached the fire doors and pushed them open hesitantly. Lying on the floor a few feet in front of him was a small pile of yellow straw.

3

When Ryan got home he called Emily's number at school. She said hello, answered his questions, assured him many times that that nothing strange had happened to her, and finally said goodbye.

He didn't leave the house for five days. He watched television and read books, mentally prepared himself to drive back to the community center without actually doing it, got too much sleep or not enough. Finally, lying in bed with his eyes wide open at three o'clock in the morning, he decided that the other shoe wasn't going to fall, that he was safe, that he was wasting his time. He went into the city the next day and spent the evening hanging out downtown.

He was on the train back home, leaning against the wall next to the seat and watching the lights rushing past his window, when he thought he heard a familiar voice. He looked over his shoulder.

Abbie was sitting in back next to the exit door. She was asleep, and her head was leaning against someone's shoulder. When Ryan leaned back to get a closer look, he saw the girl he'd met at the ice cream shop. She ran her stubbly fingers through Abbie's hair and looked up, a thin smile on her face.

Ryan blinked, and they vanished. He never saw them again.

Rolling Bones

1

Behind the house I used to live in was a patch of woods four or five acres deep, so thick you couldn't see the other side of it except at night, when the lights from the billboards shone through the branches and marked the distance between the end of my backyard and the beginning of the street. When I was little, they seemed to be endless, and I took it for granted that even if I devoted my whole life to exploring them there would be parts I would never reach. I was fifteen years old before I started from my house and traveled clean through to the other side.

It was late on a Wednesday night, long past the time when I should have gone to sleep, and I was curled into a ball on top of my mattress. My sheets and blankets were balled up at the foot of my bed; my heart was racing for no reason, and I wanted to move my legs. I snuck out through the back door and ran out onto the grass, sprinting towards the trees, and I didn't stop running until I was far enough into the woods that I was sure nobody could see me.

The ground sloped gently downward as the trees were replaced with thick brown reeds, and I hit a wall, a stack of wooden pillars held together by concrete. I climbed it and poked my head up over the top; on the other side was the back lot of a strip mall, just big enough to hold a few cars or a delivery truck. There were three men standing in a semi-circle facing the building, concentrating intently on the ground in between them. They all wore jeans and T-shirts, like mine but ripped and stained and thinned out, work clothes. One of them shook his wrist and waved his arm, and something small and hard to see bounced off the wall.

They hadn't seen me yet. It was only right then that I started getting nervous; I was about to run home, when suddenly I saw another guy running towards us from an adjoining parking lot. He was wearing a black motorcycle jacket and had short brown hair, locked into place with too much hairspray. He was pale but sweating like a pig, his eyes wide open. The other three men looked in his direction. They kept playing their game, throwing the dice and scooping them up again.

"One more time," the man in the jacket said as he approached. "I've thought about it, and I want to play one more time."

They stopped what they were doing. This is where it's difficult for me to be sure what really happened. I only put it all together a long time afterwards, and it's hard to tell where I might be imagining things. But as I remember it now, in the silence after the man in the motorcycle jacket spoke, the air froze.

I didn't wait to see what was going to happen - I dropped back down into the swamp, turned around and ran home.

2

A year later, my parents got divorced and we sold the house. Developers came in and leveled everything. The land where the woods had been was split down the middle between new houses and an expansion of the shopping center, and the strip mall was absorbed into the rest of the design, a huge industrial park surrounded by storefronts. I went there once, late on an especially empty Saturday night after I got my driver's license. I was walking along the sidewalk underneath the canopy, when, moving from one island to another, I passed an alley and turned my head. A security guard was standing there, leaning against the back of a white van. I kept walking, and a yellow light came to life above his head like a halo as I went past. I didn't come back, not that night and not for a long time afterwards.

Two years later, I got my first real job, working at a music shop. The shop was on the south corner of the same alley I hadn't gone into two years earlier; the location was actually the first thing that popped into my head when Chris mentioned the place. Chris was a friend of mine who'd graduated a couple of years ahead of me. He managed the store now. The job wasn't hard at all, even easier than he described and definitely easier than working for my Dad, even if it didn't pay as well.

There was another guy, Mike, that he always did shifts with, with me making three. It seemed strange to me at first that there were so many of us in the store at the same time. There was hardly enough work for one person. I didn't know why Chris didn't just replace Mike with me, or schedule Mike at times when he didn't have to deal with him personally. If hiring me was Chris' way to shake up conversation in the store, then it didn't work. I didn't speak up very often, didn't change the rhythm.

Mike was going to be a cop. He was going to get going on the training once he'd padded his bank account a little. He talked about it all the time.

"So they're both packing shotguns, and my eyes are already fucking bulging after that, but then they open the trunk and they have a fucking machine-gun. It costs three grand and it's optional, but every fucking squad car has one."

"What do you need a machine gun for if your job is to hand out traffic tickets?"

"You don't know what's going to happen. You want to have it."

"I know you want to have it. You're insane. There's no way every cop cares about that crap enough to fill out three grand."

"Of course they care about that crap. Why else does a person want to be a cop?"

"So you can wave a gun around?"

"Yeah, so you can wave a gun around."

There was a big grin plastered on Mike's face the whole time. Every day was like that.

3

"Arcades and strip clubs, Chris. That's all there's going to be."

"And bars."

"I don't drink. And I'm a night owl. What am I going to do when the only thing for me to do after midnight is play pinball?"

"Strip clubs. Or the city."

"City isn't getting any livelier, and I don't go to strip clubs. We need some fucking culture around here."

"You have a problem with naked women, Mike?"

"How do you feel about naked women, Janet?"

I straightened a poster hanging on the wall before I stepped out the door.

"Love them to pieces. Goodnight guys."

I was leaving early that night. It took about twenty minutes to reach my Dad's house. Walking by, I saw three guys standing in the alley. I didn't look at them twice, didn't think about them. The only thing I did was walk by a little faster.

When I got home my dad wasn't there, and I was glad. I had no reason to want to talk to him; the only conversation we had going anymore was why I was working minimum wage for somebody else when I could be making ten an hour for him, and the only reason he wanted to talk about that was so he could yell at me about college some more. My Dad owned a landscaping business. I'd spent the last five summers doing paperwork for him, but I didn't find out that was supposed to be my career until after I graduated. It wasn't a fair fight - he had no chance of keeping me home. The only thing he could do was make my life miserable until September.

Later on it started raining, heavy sheets of water, thunder and lightning. The house was empty; I sat on the porch all night and watched it come down. When I went back to the store the next day, Chris was there and Mike wasn't. Chris was upset; he wouldn't say what about at first, but he started talking right after his first break and he didn't stop. Mike had gotten arrested last night. It had something to do with his driving, but when I tried to get the details Chris changed the subject.

"I don't know what this is going to do for everything he was planning. He's acting like he never wanted to be a cop at all, like he was just playing pretend. And now he's not here today. This job isn't much, but at least it's something. I can't cover for him forever. Does he just want to get fired now?

"He finally seemed like he knew what he was doing, like he had a plan. Something that he really wanted. I just wish I knew if he really made a mistake or if he did it on purpose, if he was just fucking around and threw it all away now just because he felt like it."

He was like that all the way through lunch. He got quiet for a while around four o'clock, then he started talking about something else.

"You know those guys who hang out in the alley next door?"

I nodded my head.

"They're there all the time. Hours every day, every night. Nobody ever bothers them. When I left the store last night after I closed, when it was still pouring, I turned around and I saw them, right when the lightning struck, and they weren't there. Right when that lightning struck, they disappeared, and when the lightening was gone they were there again. They just weren't fucking there, only…"

He paused before he continued.

"… it was like… right around the edges of where they were, it was a different color… like a fire burning…"

He looked at my face, looked away again. There was twenty minutes left until the store closed. Chris didn't say a word the whole time.

4

He didn't bring up the alley the next day, or the day after that, or ever again directly, but he did talk about Mike, more and more often over the next few weeks. Whether or not he was going to be a cop, whether or not he was going to go to jail, what grades he'd gotten, what chances he had, college stuff, job stuff, everything. Mike only came back to the store once - I was dealing with a customer while Chris was on his lunch break, and when I glanced up at the front windows I saw the two of them talking out on the sidewalk. They had smiles on their faces, and everything seemed to be fine, but when Chris came back in he couldn't sit still. He walked from one end of the store to the other, like the ground was going to open under his feet and swallow him up if he stayed in one place for too long.

Even after that, I didn't really start getting worried until a few days later. Chris was talking on the phone, answering questions. He reached for a piece of paper on the desk in front of him and flipped it over. I saw a burn mark on his palm, near his thumb, a soft, dark brown square with a white dot in the middle of it.

When he noticed me looking at him he hung up the phone and turned away.

"Chris?"

He wouldn't answer me.

5

When I got home, my Dad still wasn't there. I hung up my jacket, went upstairs, and fell into bed.

It was on the walk home that I remembered seeing the dice players before. It just hit me mid-step, not a whole picture, but something, and just laying there I could feel it, the loose connections flying like tiny firecrackers. It took me half an hour just to decide that it wasn't my imagination, that the three men playing in the alley now were the same ones I'd seen three years ago, standing in the same place, moving the same way, wearing the same three faces that I couldn't quite picture. Three years wasn't that long, I knew that. Not enough time to get old in, but too much to go by without something changing.

The boys at the store weren't anything to me. Two friends, and it isn't that hard for me to make friends when I feel like it. I wondered where I'd be in three years, if I'd be the same or different. I fell asleep.

When I opened my eyes again it was almost midnight. What I did next might seem strange, but there weren't very many things in my life that summer. People who shouldn't have been all that important took up more room than they would have otherwise. And anyway, I hadn't sneaked out of the house in a really long time.

I went back downstairs and saw the car in our driveway. Everything was quiet; my Dad was asleep. I got behind the wheel.

6

I parked in the far corner of the parking lot and approached the alley. The three of them were still there, playing their game. There was also a woman with long black hair, not part of the group but standing close to them, playing with them, and another man, leaning against the wall nearby.

As I got closer, the man turned towards me. He took a quick look at my face, then turned away and stared at the wall. I leaned next to him and waited nervously. Nobody was saying anything; there was no noise except the traffic. I watched the game and wished for lightning.

The black-haired woman turned around and walked away from the circle. I saw her face as she walked past - she was a few years older than I was. She looked like she'd just seen a friend die.

The man next to me glanced at her, marginally interested.

"How'd you do?" he said.

"I won," she whispered, and left.

The man stepped up to the circle, and I took his place on the wall. He didn't play for very long, just a few minutes before he turned around and walked away, his expression unchanged.

I stepped up.

"We've seen you before."

I nodded my head, and felt the air grow cold around me.

"You weren't so frightened then."

My surroundings fell away - everything was a dark cave, hanging like the sky overhead. I couldn't tell how they were dressed, how old they were, where one ended and the other two began; there was only a single pair of eyes, marking their center.

It spoke again. Its voice was warm and comforting.

"You can ask me a question," it said. "You don't have to play, just to ask a question."

I couldn't think of what I wanted to say. My brain felt warm and soupy, the disconnection and confusion in my memory moving into the present.

It was funny; it almost sounded like something my father would say.

My fingers started itching. I became suddenly aware that I could walk away, that I didn't have to play. I tried to think of something else to ask, but realized that I had no more questions.

The dice burnt my skin as I released them from my hand.

Another Saturday Night

1

They've existed for as long as we've had the words to describe them. Hidden corners, forbidden caves, fortresses on mountaintops too tall for men to climb. Gathering places for dark powers.

In the present day, they mostly take the form of hotel bars.

2

Charlie smiled and kept talking. He had a beautiful voice, corny like your favorite uncle on Christmas day but smooth and lilting, easy to pay attention to.

"… and I said I'm just glad I don't have to take requests tonight…"

The brunette laughed kindly, as though a child had made the joke. Most people meeting her for the first time are surprised at how easy she is to get along with. It's only after a long association that she begins to seem pretentious, like a billionaire who wears jeans everywhere.

"All right then. I need to get out of here, good seeing you. I feel bad I can't stop by more often."

"No rest for the wicked, right?"

She smiled back like she'd never heard that joke before. "You got it. Good night, Abby."

Abby was a beautiful girl, somewhere around eighteen years old. She had blue eyes and blonde hair.

"Good night."

The brunette vanished in a whiff of sulfur.

"God, she's a bitch."

"She probably just heard you say that."

"Yeah, well, maybe I should've said it a little louder to make sure. I have my sponsor."

She looked over his shoulder. A doughy woman in a green sweater and black sweat pants was sitting in a chair in the corner. Abby smiled at her and she smiled back. She had a flat face and dark eyes that cut right through you. There were a few others that you could see. A group of men in identical trench coats were playing pool, and a skinny woman with a black cat on her shoulder was looking out the window, watching it snow. Every so often a snake seemed to slide across the carpet from one corner of the room to the other. Still, it was a slow night.

Abby and Charlie had always gotten along. They had both been human relatively recently; Charlie had died, while Abby's situation was more complicated. The others didn't always know what to make of them, so they kept each other company.

"I don't know why you kids have to use language like that anyway."

"You're a fuddy-duddy." She laughed and said it again. "Fuddy-duddy."

"I'm sure I am, young lady."

"When did you die, anyway?"

"1967. The Monkees had just hit number one."

"You know they were fake, right?"

"The songs weren't fake, that's the only part I care about. Are you still in love with that drug addict?"

"You mean Kurt Cobain? Old man?"

"Yes I am and yes that's who I meant."

"Forever and ever."

The television hanging in the corner came on. The trench coats stopped playing and the black cat turned its head slightly.

"What's that?" Abby asked.

"I'm not sure. Probably somebody showing off."

Poor people from the small housing project on the northern side of the street standing on the concrete median that divides the road, waiting for the traffic to let up so they can walk to the grocery store. Late winter evening, snow on the ground, salt on the sidewalks that wasn't there the last time Jeremy made the trip home. He just had dinner with his parents. His older brother had made a surprise visit; they'd all eaten together and talked about what was going on with him. He'd finished his engineering degree last year and bought himself a plasma TV as a reward for his first full twelve months of employment. Mom and Dad were proud enough to burst, they talked more about the television than the fucking job.

Jeremy had almost finished his degree in counseling and was thirty thousand dollars in debt. On the drive up the number had run through his head over and over again like a horse on a carousel. Now it was just sitting there. He'd meant to ask about borrowing some money, and he still wasn't sure if he'd lost the nerve or had an attack of pride. He was angry about something, he could feel it in his fingers.

He takes the ramp to the expressway; he drives, he drives, he drives. A pack of motorcycles blast past him on both sides, bobbing and weaving through the lanes. He taps on the brakes, gripped the wheel a little tighter as they disappeared.

It kept going, but it was clear now that it was going to take a while for anything to happen. The attention of everyone at the bar began to wane.

"So what's the point, exactly?" Abby asked.

"Not sure yet," Charlie said. "It might become clear later."

It was a Wednesday night. Jeremy didn't come from a drinking family; he had a habit of picking the wrong bar and refusing to admit it until too much of the night had gone by to go somewhere else. The place he found himself in now had Rat Pack pictures on the walls and dark green curtains filling the windows. There were three other people there, not counting the bartender, a man with a beard staring at his glass as though he wanted to hurt it and two women not quite old enough to be his mother, talking and laughing like best friends sharing a dirty joke.

The skinny lady in the turtleneck laughs at him. She means to be friendly but it pisses him off anyway. "Well I guess you're not going to make much doing that, honey."

No shit. "Yeah, it's kind of a dues paying thing."

"So you got to do this before you head up to the North Shore and make your money listening to rich people talk about their problems."

Fuck that. "Yeah, I guess."

"Well, that's not so bad, then. You'll come out of it with some stories, anyway. You got any stories?"

That afternoon, he'd come back to the house after his lunch break and found one of his residents waving a broken bottle at his roommate. The one with the bottle was named Freddy; he had glasses and occasionally believed that he was a famous heart surgeon. Freddy's roommate was named Mike; he was very quiet and liked to drink the good root beer that came in glass bottles. Mike had always struck Jeremy as the kind of guy who could just as easily be living on his own with a social worker checking on him, but he'd been in freak-out mode today, sitting on the floor and babbling while Freddy swung the jagged glass past his face over and over again.

A man in black leather driving gloves appeared out of nowhere and sat down next to Abby and Charlie.

"Sitting in a bar watching a TV with a guy sitting in a bar on it. Makes me wonder if I need to get a life."

His voice bled and rattled.

"Hey, I got an idea."

He clacked his teeth together and suddenly Jeremy and the two women were sitting at the empty stools on the other side of the bar, continuing their conversation as though nothing had happened.

"I mean, it only went on for a little bit, there was a security guard there and we got everybody separated and back in their rooms. But we got lucky, somebody could've gotten hurt."

"My god. Does that kind of thing happen often?"

"Well, not usually, that's the whole deal. The reason they keep the place open is because they don't know what else to do with the property and it's not worth enough to bother selling. The only people they put there are the ones that they don't want in a larger facility, but because the staff's so small they don't want any huge safety risks either. Except with an incident…" Incident wasn't one of his words, it was one of theirs, but he found himself using it more and more often. "…an incident like this, everybody's worried about liability. They might have to close the place."

"What's going to happen to the inmates?"

"They're not inmates, they're residents, it's not a prison…"

He doesn't realize he's being rude until it's too late to apologize.

"They're out. That's it."

"Where will they stay? Do any of them have family?"

"No, if there was family willing to take them they wouldn't be where they are."

No comment from either one of them, they didn't get it.

"They aren't going to have housing. They will be homeless."

"Are you really sure this is what's going to happen?"

Yes, he really was sure.

"Really?"

Yes, really.

"I can't believe that. That can't be right."

The man in the driving gloves clacks his teeth again. They reappear on the television screen.

They talk for a few more minutes. They still don't believe him. He realizes that he's getting angry and decides to leave.

There's a karaoke stage in the far corner of the bar, a black box with a microphone hanging in front of it. It caught his eye as he stepped out the door and for the moment he thought he saw something strange, a shimmering white curtain, like sunlight reflecting off of frozen tree branches, cutting that side of the room off from the part of the bar he'd entered.

Leaving the bar, he's wondering if he's seeing things.

"Are you doing that?" Abby asked, trying not to sound interested.

"No, he's really going crazy. Just a little bit, happens to everybody. It's not going to get really bad until the guy waving the bottle around hangs himself."

He sees it again a few days later, on the el train taking him to work. The rooftops and the windows and the doorways, everything shimmering, blinding him. The train stops; he gets off, takes the stairs down to the street, and he can see again.

There's an ambulance parked in front of the house where he works. Bystanders watch from a polite distance, old people with dogs and mothers taking their children for a walk. They whisper and Jeremy eavesdrops, but they don't know anything. He pushes past them. The front door opens and the paramedics hustle through. They're inside the ambulance before Jeremy can figure out who it is they're carrying. They know exactly what they're doing.

"Now we're cooking with gas."

Charlie pushed an empty glass towards the bartender. "We really aren't interested in talking to you."

He kept talking.

"But this is where it gets predictable, too. It's over so quickly when it goes quick, but when it goes slow they don't even notice. They just keep puttering around, always wondering what else could have happened, who they threw away that they should have kept, what they should have done that they can't do anymore, watching their last little sliver of time go down the drain while they're still trying to figure out what to do about it…"

He stopped. You could hear the wheels turning. He smiled a little wider.

"I can't believe I never thought of this before."

It's Sunday and he's driving to his parents' house again. The light is everywhere, but it's different now, focused. There are tiny little lines crossing doorways of buildings on either side of the road, and when he passes the housing project there's a barrier surrounding it. It looks like the sun is shining right out of the ground, just inside the fence.

He turns onto a side-street and parks the car. There's a bunch of kids with skateboards in the parking lot of an adjacent liquor store. They take a quick look at him before turning their attention back toward themselves.

He approaches the fence and raises his hand, holds it about an inch away from the place where the light begins. There's no pain, no change in temperature or texture, but for some reason he can go no further.

"Nobody goes everywhere, does everything. You can live in a city of ten million people but how many of them do you really know? A couple dozen if you get out a lot? You don't really live in the city, you live in a small town filled with ghosts you never meet or talk to. People live in a bubble. Inside the bubble are all the places they go before they die, outside is everything else. The whole world, almost.

"I don't even need to lay a finger on him. It's not a barrier, he's not trapped. I'm actually doing him a favor. People throw money down the drain on those psychic hotlines for shit like this and they don't even do it right.

"He was never going to go into that neighborhood. Even if he weren't a chickenshit, he'd never go in there. Why would he? He has no reason.

"Do you think he'll go crazy when he figures it out?"

He opens a road map, and he's blinded. Everything is glowing, with only a few exceptions, little dots around Chicago and little lines snaking out, following the highways. There were a few other trails that spread further out, one to either coast and another one that started near an airport and cut a gentle curve over the continent, across the ocean, past the edge of the map. He'd been to New York last summer, but he'd never left the country before.

He wonders where he's going to go, when he did make that trip. All he had to do to find out was find a globe and that'd be it. No more worrying.

"No more surprises, his whole worthless life laid out for him…"
"You don't know anything," Charlie said.

The man in the black gloves stopped laughing. He'd mostly been talking to himself, he'd forgotten that anybody else was there.

"People know that they're going to die. Everybody knows that. They do the best they can with the time they have."

"So how did you spend your time, Charlie?" He waved his hand and suddenly there was a map of the country sitting on the counter. With the exception of a few dull spots around Milwaukee, all of it was glowing.

"Never got all that far, did you champ? You were a disc jockey, right? Put records on a little spinning wheel, talked into a microphone?"

Jeremy sits in a fast food restaurant, staring out the window. He has a half-eaten sub sandwich sitting on the table in front of him; there are little pieces of lettuce scattered around it on the wrapper. He's been sitting here for almost an hour. His eyes are red and swollen. He's been having trouble sleeping. He thinks that the people behind the counter are talking about him but he isn't sure. He wonders if he's going to get kicked out.

He wraps up his sandwich, throws it out, and leaves. He sees a diagonal line cutting across the pavement, sparkling gently in the sun. He walks to the other side of the street without crossing it.

"Maybe you're right, Charlie," the man said. "It's a little traumatic right now, but time fixes everything. He'll get used to it, he'll come to terms.

"Check this out."

He's no longer sitting at the bar.

He's standing in the middle of the road. He's smiling.
"You got a problem?"
Jeremy grimaces at the sound of his voice. He keeps on smiling.
"Don't worry. There's hope."
He pushes him with both hands. Jeremy stumbles backwards, over the line. There's a wall of cold black stone where the light had been, stretching up and out as far as he can see.

3

The man in the black gloves didn't come back to the bar that evening.

128

"Goddamn it." Abby pushed her glass away from her. "I'm sorry, I know your night off is a big deal and I don't want to waste it talking about depressing shit."

Charlie shrugged. "He gets on my nerves too, but there's not much we can really do. Don't worry for my sake, though. He's an asshole, never any shortage of those."

He finished his drink.

"Almost midnight," Abby said.

"That's right. Should probably be getting back to work."

Charlie always left quietly. Abby interrupted him before he disappeared.

"Charlie?"

He reappeared, but she didn't know what to say. She looked down at her feet. Charlie put his hand on her shoulder.

"Hey, look at me for a second."

She looked up.

"It's hard now, but it gets easier. That's how it was for me anyway. Are you going to be all right?"

She nodded.

"Eventually. I know you've got to run. See you next week?"

"You got it. Listen to the radio tonight."

And he was gone.

People were starting to clear out. Abby walked over to where the woman in the green sweater was sitting.

"Can we leave?"

She nodded her head. Abby helped her to her feet and they left the bar.

They made it home a few minutes later. Home was a strange place, mostly empty space and dim colors, but Abby had a room to herself that was a little more like what she was used to. She laid down and listened to the radio.

There's got to be some kind of way out of here
Said the joker to the thief

Story Notes

The Black Plague

I was in Venice with my parents and my sister, wandering through the streets feeling lost, when I saw a stand selling plague masks. Years earlier, a friend of mine from college had a job working at a Shakespeare festival in Spring Green, Wisconsin. Spend enough time daydreaming and things come together for you.

Music for Scalpel and Prepared Piano

The title came first - I misread the name of a band on a T-shirt of a guy on the el. Story followed. My usual method is to spew out a sloppy rough draft and then spend a lot of time cutting things out. This is an extreme example of that.

The House Rock and Roll Built

I had a job as a literacy and GED tutor at a maximum security prison for teenage girls. I spent a lot of time reading *Come As You Are: An Oral History of Nirvana* with one of my students, which led to a lot of interesting conversations about drugs and creativity and art and commerce. I was a lot more polite talking with my student than I am here, which is usually how these things go.

A Black Hole In Chicago

This story ended up being less of a Raymond Chandler tribute than I'd intended - the original opening was basically "a blonde walked into my office". But I like the restaurant better. The pimp story I only heard second-hand. The "furniture up in this bitch" anecdote happened to me, unfortunately. I lived with that guy for a year.

Quiet

I wrote this at the height of the Bush administration. *24* was in its fourth season or so. My younger sister Sarah is a political operative slash superhero who's spent a lot of time in the Middle East. She tells me that she's found CIA trainees to generally be the kinds of dudes who want to get to shoot people but are scared to join the Marines. Sounds plausible to me.

Ducks

One of my neighbors in the suburb where I grew up was an Egyptian man who'd married an American woman and had gone native just about completely. Another one of my neighbors was a Jewish widow who was dearly loved by everyone in the neighborhood and threw cross-denominational Hanukkah parties at her house every year. I wrote this story solely so that I'd have somewhere to use their "ancient enemy" routine. Needed some *C.H.U.D.*, of course.

Dinosaurs

This story was originally published by Chizine, which for my money is the coolest venue for horror short stories anywhere, period, and benefitted a lot from the process of working with their editors. I've still never read any of the *Left Behind* books all the way through, but I've read all the book jackets and have to admit that a ragtag group of believers going on a suicide mission to take out the Antichrist is a pretty awesome hook.

Lake Sympathy

Long drive through northern Michigan early in the morning and here you go. Last time I checked this was my mother's favorite story that I've written.

Veronica

I once read an interview with a guy who writes crime fiction whose advice was to always put the thing the protagonist values the most in real danger and to never settle for anything less. This story was a deliberate attempt not to do that. I like this character a lot, and I have a strong feeling that she'll be turning up again.

Iowa Highway

My uncle is a trucker. It's not a career that has treated him especially well. An earlier version of this story was produced by the horror audio fiction podcast Pseudopod and was discussed in their forums, many of whom had experience in the business and whose feedback I deeply appreciate.

The Invasion

I wrote this story for an anthology with the theme of combining urban legends and UFO mythology. This was not what they were looking for. I like it anyway, even though I'm apparently the only guy in the world who's heard the one about Mountain Dew diminishing your potency.

Mario and Luigi and the Lords of the Sky

Another story written for an anthology and left stranded when it didn't get in. The Hunter S. Thompson graffiti could once be found on the far western section of the Prairie Path bike trail but I don't know if it's still there.

Dress Rehearsal

A weird pet peeve I have is the inadequate artistic treatments of real social problems, the way that *Walker, Texas Ranger* can effortlessly turn an inner city teenager's life around by kicking a gang leader in the head and then having a heart-to-heart chat with the kid in question.

Humility

Another themed anthology submission that was left stranded on the Island of Misfit Toys. The anthology had a "femme fatale" theme. This was my attempt to do a negative image of that kind of character.

Super Jesus

This story has no redeeming social value at all. It is a sick joke and shame on you if you enjoyed it. The situation is made worse by the fact that I have a dear friend name Jon who is just finishing his time in the seminary, a fact that I sincerely and hilariously failed to connect to the contents of this story until long after it was finished. Also, the green super bunny costume was mine as a nine-year old. There are pictures.

Red Rover

This was one of the first short stories I wrote when I was in college and made it a goal to start getting my writing published. I don't have much to say about it now except that I'm happy to empathize less with the protagonist than I used to, and that when you're under twenty-one, home from school on break, and don't drink you have to squeeze blood from a stone sometimes to find entertainment.

Rolling Bones

This was the first short story I ever got published. I never got paid for it. The website that bought it was supported by banner ads for goth chick porn sites - it seemed like a decent enough business model to me but they went out of business anyway. The backyard mentioned in this story is based on the one behind the house I grew up in.

Another Saturday Night

I'm mostly gonna leave this one alone, except to say that if you like Charlie then I'd encourage you to stay tuned. I have plans for Mr. Harmer.

I've been blessed in my life with more wonderful people than I deserve or expect to remember to mention here. Thank you to everyone from whom I've stolen an aspect of their appearance, an anecdote, a story, or a personality trait. Thank you to my parents, who took good care of a weird kid who spent too much time in his room typing, and who still do. Thank you to my sister for being my favorite person on the face of the earth. Thank you to everyone in my enormous extended family, but in particular thank you to my uncle Rob and uncle Dan and my cousin Alex for being fans, to my aunt Sasha and cousins Azure and Bianca for being radiant and wonderful, and to my uncle Dick for helping me with my website and for showing the weird kid mentioned above that the world is a big cool weird place with lots of stuff in it worth checking out. Thank you to Ms. Edwards and Phil Shields, who should notice that they are the only participants in my formal education mentioned here and be duly flattered. Thank you to the members of the Townhouse C diaspora, to Hunter C. Eden and Alex Collier who are other badass authors you should look up, to Brian Graham, and to Valerie Toth whom I miss and who should send me a goddamn e-mail. And thank you to all my Chicago writer friends, everybody from Kate the Greats and Twilight Tales and Cult Fiction, CSE Cooney and Patty Templeton and Tina Jens and Eric Cherry and Jude Mire and Mike Penkas and Mike Martinez and Frank Stascik and Reina Hardy and Joshua Doetsch and whomever I'm forgetting who should please forgive me. We're all gonna be big stars.

Also thank you from the bottom of my heart to everyone who made the marketing and distribution of this book possible. Without them the party does not happen. Specifically:

Debbi Daniel-Wayman
Michael Detzner
Dan Detzner
Dick Detzner & Sasha Rubel- www.detzner.com
Rob Detzner
Tom "It's just sex" Tancredi
Georgianne Detzner
Sarah Detzner
Barbara Stob
Charlotte Hammond- www.charlottehammond.com
Alexei Collier
Reina Hardy
Matthew Stewart
Laura Mariani
Jude W. Mire
Joshua Alan Doetsch
Michael Penkas
Eric Cherry- Soundspainful.com
Adam Daniel-Wayman
CSE Cooney

I hope you enjoyed the book. You can keep tabs on what I'm doing by Liking Brendan Detzner (author) on Facebook and by checking out my website at www.brendandetzner.com, and you can meet me in person at the monthly Bad Grammar Theater shows in Chicago and other events around the city. I'm the big dude with the shaved head. Don't hesitate to introduce yourself.

www.ingramcontent.com/pod-product-compliance
Lightning Source LLC
Chambersburg PA
CBHW051844170626
46807CB00003B/1349